THE UNDERGROUND, FREEDOM'S ROAD
AND OTHER UPSTATE TALES

THE UNDERGROUND, FREEDOM'S ROAD AND OTHER UPSTATE TALES

By ARCH MERRILL

Cover art and Creek logo
by Charlotte Lewis

ISBN: 0-932771-50-5

Creek Books
Division of Nor-Del Productions, Ltd.
PO Box 93262
Rochester, New York 14692-8262

Contents

List of Illustrations

THE UNDERGROUND, FREEDOM'S ROAD
AND OTHER UPSTATE TALES

Chapter 1

Preface and Acknowledgments

The major part of this book deals with the story of the Underground Railroad, the secret network by which thousands of runaway Negro slaves were spirited to freedom before the Civil War.

The first chapter of this book tells why it is not a complete, documented history of the Underground's operations in Central-Western New York. Such a work is impossible to write. Few Underground stations or their "agents" can be positively identified. Any researcher runs against a wall of secrecy and silence.

But despite the traditions and the legends, there are many incidents and personalities belonging to the movement that can be verified. The Underground formed a dramatic chapter in our national history.

There were "Freedom Riders" in the 1850s, as in the 1960s. There were "racial crises" and emotions ran high then as now—but under entirely different circumstances.

Following the Underground section of this book are several chapters based on events related to the Civil War. The last chapter tells the almost forgotten story of America's last great gold rush and the part Central-Western New York "sourdoughs" played in that stampede to the Klondike country in the 1890s.

In gathering the material for this book, the author received generous help from many sources. My thanks go to the Local History Divisions of the Rochester and Syracuse Public Libraries, to the Grosvenor Library in Buffalo and to the Wood Memorial Library and Museum in Canandaigua.

Also to Mrs. Harry Russell of Le Roy, Mrs. Julia G. Pierce, Cattaraugus County Historian; J. Sheldon Fisher, Ontario County Historian; Harry S. Douglass, Wyoming County Historian; Mrs. Florence Lee, Monroe County Historian; Mrs. Dorothy S. Facer, Wayne County Historian; Mrs. Marie Preston, Livingston County Historian and her assistant, Miss Anna E. Patchett; Niagara County Historian Clarence O. Lewis, Orleans County Historian Cary H. Lattin, Mrs. Inez M. Shear, Allegany County Historian.

William Heidt Jr., of the DeWitt Historical Society and Sydney H. Gallwey, both of Ithaca; Dr. Arthur E. May, superintendent of the Harriet Tubman Home, Auburn; Mrs. Charles Lewis of Seneca Falls, Lewis H. Bishop of Warsaw, Mrs. Eleanor C. Kalsbeck, Henrietta Town Historian; Miss Alta M. Fisher, Perinton Town Historian, Mrs. Edna Plumb, Macedon Town Historian; Miss Katherine H. Billings, Albion Town Historian, Herbert J. Ellis, Canandaigua City Historian.

Clayton J. Scoins of East Pembroke, Miss Doris Smith of Mohawk, N.Y., Howard W. Tellier and John Schuyler of Naples, Ralph C. Jackman of North Cohocton, Mrs. Mabel E. Oaks of Oaks Corners, Miss Josephine Johnson of Geneva, Jay D. Barnes of Penn Yan, Miss Cora Warrant and William J. Babcock of Rochester, Frank Connor of Hemlock, Mrs. Virginia Hawley of Pultneyville, Mrs. Irilene Millan Oakleaf of Williamson and Mrs. Kenneth Werder of Honeoye.

Chapter 2

A Vast, Silent Conspiracy

What was the Underground Railroad? It wasn't a railroad at all. It had no rails, no locomotives, no fixed schedules. It did not have hundreds of "stations" and hundreds of "conductors," many of them in Central-Western New York.

And it "carried" thousands of passengers. It was Jim Crowism in reverse. For only men, women and children with dark skins traveled the invisible road which followed the North Star from the land of bondage to the shores of freedom.

The Underground Railroad was the name given a vast, silent conspiracy, conceived and operated by humanitarians who defied a law of the land because they believed it violated the inherent right of human beings to be free.

It operated like a thief in the night. It had to. For it was engaged in stealing property valued into the millions. To this day all but the boldest and most prominent operators remain anonymous. It had no formal organization. It kept few records and its operators were not given to writing memoirs.

They were law breakers. After the Fugitive Slave Law was drastically toughened by an amendment, part of the Compromise of 1850, anyone who harbored runaway slaves or in any way hampered their recapture was subject to heavy fines, even imprisonment.

Although the Underground was operating long before 1850, the high tide of traffic on the Freedom Road followed the passage of the hated law. That human stream lasted for a decade until the outbreak of the Civil War. After that it dwindled to a trickle. The Underground was no longer needed.

Despite the secrecy and legends which shroud the operations of the Underground, a dramatic story emerges, a story of daring, fortitude, ingenuity, mystery-and considerable fanaticism.

Out of the past come pictures of runaways plodding along in the darkness with only the North Star to guide them. Sometimes the slave catchers were hot on their trail. The fugitives hid in woods, in swamps, caves and in the tall weeds.

They swam rivers and rode rafts and logs to the free shore. They reached havens along the line, known to them through the grapevine which wound through the plantation kingdom.

Slaves were shipped in packing boxes. A Negro mother and her young daughter rode all the long way from Washington, D.C. to Warsaw, hidden for 22 days and 22 nights in a wooden box on a wagon. "Uncle Billy" Marks of Naples carried many a fugitive from his station to the next in one of his hearses. Sometimes they were concealed in coffins.

The runaways were stowed away under produce in wagons and in hay racks. They were secreted behind piles of wood on lake docks. They were tucked among trunks and boxes in baggage cars through the connivance of railroad employes, often with the approval of the officials of the road. They walked the roads, each carrying a hoe, an ax or other tool as if they were workmen going from job to job. When his mother, a tiny woman, became ill and could walk no farther, a Negro youth put her in a bag, which he carried for miles over his shoulder until he found sanctuary.

Men wearing Quaker bonnets and long dresses and women disguised as men were driven in heavily curtained carriages to lake docks and then rowed out to waiting Canada-bound ships. Sewing circles along the line kept disguises on hand for emergencies.

Refugees were hidden in homes, in barns, stables, basement vaults, attics, secret chambers, root cellars, corn cribs, hay stacks, in churches, even in church belfries.

Who ran this secret railroad? Many people, all sorts of people, white and Negro. They were aristocrats and humble farmers, intellectuals and unlettered workmen, anyone who had compassion for the oppressed and the hunted. They risked their liberty, their reputations and their personal safety to help weary, bedraggled, frightened Negro slaves along the freedom road.

Wealthy and prominent folk braved social ostracism and shrugged off such epithets as "crackpots" and "nigger lovers" while they poured their time and money into the cause. The Quakers, always the friends of the underdog, were in the vanguard of the Underground movement.

Ghosts ride the Underground. We see ugly, turbaned, lion-hearted Harriet Tubman leading 300 of her people out of the land of bondage. We see the eloquent and self-educated former slave, Frederick Douglass, opening his home to runaways, putting them aboard Canada-bound ships, pleading the abolition cause with voice and pen. We see Allegany County–born Calvin Fairbank enduring 17 gruesome years in Southern prisons for helping Negroes to escape.

The story of the Underground is rich in drama. There were riots, spectacular rescue, rescue attempts that failed, some murders, a few suicides. Some slave hunters were not treated gently.

A mass of myths becloud the story of the Underground. As time went on, many an ordinary coal bin or fruit cellar became in popular fancy a hiding place for fugitive slaves. Most of the tales of secret tunnels used as Underground passageways have been exploded.

The most unlikely story of all is that some stations were marked by some elaborate emblem or sign. The operators of the Underground were far too shrewd to leave any such tell-tale markings along their secret trails.

Despite the myths and the legends, Operation Underground was a significant and exciting chapter in American history. In it Central and Western New York played no minor part.

Chapter 3

In the Early Years

Around 1831 a Negro slave fled a Kentucky plantation and, leaping into the Ohio River, began swimming toward the Ohio shore.

His master gave chase in a boat. He could see ahead of him a woolly head bobbing in the water and watched his property wade ashore to the freedom-loving Ohio town of Ripley. There all trace of him was lost. The planter never saw his slave again.

The Kentuckian scratched his head and in his perplexity uttered a phrase which was to live in history: "He must gone on an *underground road.*"

"Underground road"—the name caught on and because the first American steam railroad had just been completed, it was twisted into "the Underground Railroad."

That was the legendary birth of the name of the invisible line which led from servitude to liberty. The word went into the language and became a generic term for undercover movements.

But long before that, slaves were running away from their masters and finding sanctuary in Northern centers.

As early as 1786 a Virginia planter of some military renown complained, after the escape of a slave from his estate and a neighbor's similar loss, that an organization of Philadelphia Quakers was sheltering runaway Negroes. The irate planter was George Washington.

In 1804 the Pennsylvania town of Columbia rose en masse to defy a master seeking a runaway slave who had found asylum there. The planter went home, empty handed.

Back in 1815 Negroes in considerable numbers were escaping from the South through Ohio. The flow steadily increased, for it was a short cut to freedom.

Meanwhile many Negroes, who had been given free papers by their masters, were drifting Northward. Many others stayed in the South, to the annoyance of the planters. The border city of Baltimore was a center to which the freed Negroes flocked in droves.

In the late years of the 18th Century and the early years of the 19th there was a growing sentiment in the South against slavery. But the widespread use of the cotton gin, invented by a Yankee, Eli Whitney, built up "the Cotton Kingdom" in the Deep South and changed the economic pattern of the region. The value of Negro field hands was tremendously enhanced and the anti-slavery movement was sharply arrested.

The freedmen on both sides of the Mason-Dixon line were to have important roles in the operations of the Underground Railroad.

* * *

It is noteworthy that the settlers of Central-Western New York included many Southerners who brought their slaves with them. The majority of them were Marylanders, lured to the Genesee Country by the promotions of the grandiose land agent, Charles Williamson. As the representative of a British syndicate headed by Sir William

Pulteney, his job was to settle a million wilderness acres.

One of the first arrivals was Col. Peregrine Fitzhugh, a Maryland aristocrat, who came in 1799 with a cavalcade of 27 covered wagons and more than a score of slaves. He settled on the heights above scenic Sodus Bay east of Sodus Point. Fitzhugh, who later moved to Geneva, soon freed his slaves. Other landed gentlemen followed suit. Descendants of these freedmen still live in the area.

Land agent Williamson experimented in Negro colonization by allowing the freed slaves land on the Pulteney holdings, settling 80 of them on his own plot. The colonies lasted only a few years.

Another Southern settler, of a different stripe then Fitzhugh, one Capt. William Helm of Prince George County, Va., came in 1800 with an overseer and some 70 slaves. He bought a 100-acre tract at the head of Sodus Bay near Port Glasgow on what in recent years was known as the Catchpole farm.

Helm did not stay long at Sodus Bay. After returning to Virginia for his family, he moved his slave farm to Bath, where he purchased a large tract which he named Meringo. Thomas Helm, also a former Revolutionary War captain, joined his brother in Bath. The brothers did not find slave holding profitable or popular in the Steuben County shire town, where both are buried.

One of the Helm slaves, Austin Steward, ran away from the Bath colony and in later years described William Helm as a brutal and overbearing master. Steward recorded his memoirs in a book titled *Twenty Two Years a Slave and Forty Years a Freeman.*

Steward, a man of parts, came to Rochester in 1816 and ran a store while helping conduct a school for young Negroes. In 1830, with the backing of Everard Peck and other Rochester liberals, he established a colony for his people at Wilberforce, Ontario, Canada. After seven years Steward returned to Rochester, penniless. Friends set him up in business again. He spent his last years in Canandaigua, where he wrote his book.

Lyons was the home of several slave holders in the early times. John Cole and his wife, an English lay preacher, are said to have brought slaves from Maryland to Lyons in 1779. Some Negroes are buried on the old Cole farm.

A more prominent slave holder and land owner in Lyons was Capt. Daniel Dorsey who in 1797 left Frederick County, Maryland, for a 1,600-acre estate which he had bought from Williamson. He kept over 40 slaves on his property south of the village on the Geneva turnpike where he built a fine mansion. Dorsey found slave holding unprofitable and liberated all his Negroes.

In 1924 a cemetery with unmarked stones was discovered on the east bank of the Canandaigua Outlet. It is believed to be the burial place of Dorsey slaves, some of whom intermarried with those on the Bennett farm in Phelps.

According to Lyons tradition, a Negro, known as "Old Wall" and reputedly an escaped slave, lived in a log hut on a small stream on the Montezuma Road east of Lyons where he made his living by hunting and fishing.

It is recorded that in 1810 Samuel Mummy sold his property on the east side of Broad Street in Lyons, along with his "coloured chattels" and returned to Maryland.

Phelps, which was to become fertile soil for the abolitionist cause, also had its slave holders. In 1800 Archibald and Zebedee Beall, brothers, brought several slaves from Maryland to land they bought northwest of the village. Archibald and his wife are buried at Five Waters near

Phelps, but brother Zeb, who was a bachelor, returned to Maryland at an early date, taking his most valuable slaves with him.

Among the Beall slaves was Sarah Countee and her four children, one of whom, John, died in 1886 at a great age. He lived in a little house on the original Beall land and for 60 years dug the graves in the Old Cemetery in Phelps.

Other Maryland families that brought slaves to the Town of Phelps were the Baggerlys, the Fergusons and the Shekells. John Shekell, one of the earliest settlers in Clifton Springs, set free his three slaves and provided homes for them.

Geneva, "an elegant and salubrious village," also had its slave holders. Robert Scott, a friend of Col. Robert Troup, Williamson's successor as the Pulteney land agent, in his will freed his slaves and bequeathed to each a sum of money. In the Towns of Seneca and Fayette freedom certificates are recorded for the slaves of Robert S. Rose and Judge John Nicholas, Virginia patricians, who established estates and elegant homes in the area in 1801.

The Bogerts, another Southern family transplanted to Geneva, kept slaves, for they advertised a runaway in 1803.

Rochester's first white settler, the bigamous Ebenezer "Indian" Allen, owned slaves. The founder of the city which bears his name, Col. Nathaniel Rochester, brought 10 slaves in the cavalcade which set out in 1810 from Hagerstown, Md., for Dansville in the new Genesee Country.

Records show that some of the Negroes were liberated in Dansville. The others may have been given their freedom before the Colonel left Maryland. At any rate all were freed and one of the motives that impelled Rochester to come North was his abhorrence of slavery.

His land-speculator partners, Charles Carroll and William Fitzhugh, also were slave holders. Whether Carroll freed his human chattels on his arrival in Williamsburg in 1815 is undetermined. But it is known that Fitzhugh brought seven young slaves with his family when they moved into the mansion at Hampton Corners. Slave holding was a way of life in the Maryland whence the three partners came to the Genesee.

Slavery never took firm root in Upstate soil. Use of slaves was not practical in this climate and public settlement in region largely settled by New Englanders was against slavery.

In 1789 a state law provided that all children born in slavery were declared free. On July 5, 1827, every slave in New York State was emancipated by law.

At that time, Wayne county annals show that the Rev. George D. Phelps, a Williamson Episcopal clergyman, owned two slaves and the Martins at Pultneyville still owned Negroes they had brought from Pennsylvania.

*   *   *

The abolition movement was catching hold in the North. Even in the 1820s Levi Coffin, the Cincinnati Quaker and the unofficial head of the Underground Railroad, had his network going full blast, and escaped slaves were pouring into Ohio, Illinois and Indiana.

In New England the fires of abolitionism were being lighted by William Lloyd Garrison, who began publishing his fearless journal, *The Liberator,* in Boston in 1831, by Wendell Phillips and others.

The abolition movement spread to Central-Western

New York where many county and town anti-slavery societies were organized. The Underground was in operation, despite the hostility of conservatives and the indifference of the general public.

New York State's pillar of abolitionism was the rich reformer, Gerrit Smith, whose purse was always open to the cause and whose Peterboro home welcomed all fugitives who came that way.

Another mainstay of the cause was Myron Holley, who lived in Rochester from 1837 until his death in 1841 and who had previously resided in Canandaigua and Lyons.

He was active in all reform movements but abolition was dearest to his heart. He founded in Rochester an abolitionist paper, after selling his farm on the Genesee to finance the enterprise. He is credited with being the first to suggest a national Liberty Party.

Holley split with the Garrisonians, who believed the issue could be settled through "moral suasion." Holley wanted it decided at the polls. Had he lived to see the flowering of the Underground, he would have been one of its leaders. Perhaps before he died he secretly helped slaves to escape.

As the Cotton Kingdom grew and gained political power, its clamor for an extension of slavery into new territory was intensified by the accession of a vast new domain through the successful war with Mexico.

The march of events precipitated a great debate which began in earnest in 1850, a debate which was not to end until Appomattox.

Chapter 4

"That Damnable Law"

It has been believed that the Missouri Compromise, guided through Congress by Henry Clay in 1820, had settled the limits of slavery for all time. Under the Compromise slavery was legalized in the new state of Missouri but not elsewhere west of the Mississippi River or north of the 36–30 longitude parallel.

So in 1850 the two aging Senate giants, Clay and Daniel Webster, with the help of young Stephen A. Douglas, got a new compromise law passed.

It made territorial concessions on the slavery issue to both North and South—but it contained a tough new Fugitive Slave Act.

The compromise package was signed by President Millard Fillmore, the bland Buffalo politico who had been regarded in his home state as an anti-slavery man. The measure was intended to end all threat of civil war. It merely postponed the conflict a decade.

The Fugitive Slave section, tossed into the package as a sop to the slave-holding South, made the Northern abolitionists see red. It rallied many moderates to their side. A mild mannered York State Quaker exclaimed: "We will never obey that damnable law."

It gave strong impetus to the Underground Railroad

14

over which poured a mounting stream of dark-skinned humanity following the North Star.

The fugitive slave measure of 1850 was flouted in the North as effectively, if not as openly, as was the whiskey tax in Pennsylvania in the late 18th Century and the prohibition law throughout the land in the 20th Century.

It was an unjust and inhumane law. It was an affront to all lovers of liberty.

For under its provisions a suspected runaway slave could be seized and shackled wherever found, denied a trial by jury or the right to hire a lawyer or call witnesses—and be dragged back into bondage.

Any federal commissioner or judge could issue a certificate for the arrest or removal of a slave. If the arrest was made without process the claimant merely had to take the fugitive before a commissioner who could summarily decide the case.

The slave could not testify in his own behalf. Ownership could be determined by a simple affidavit presented by a claimant. The law gave a commissioner authority to summon a posse to seize a fugitive.

The refusal of a United States marshal or deptuy to execute a commissioner's certificate meant a $1,000 fine and failure to prevent the escape of a Negro after arrest made the marshal liable for the value—which could run into four figures.

Anyone who obstructed an arrest, who rescued, harbored or concealed a runaway slave was subject to a $1,000 maximum fine, six months imprisonment and liability for damages at the rate of $1,000 per fugitive lost.

The commissioner received a $10 fee if he issued a warrant. If the case was dismissed, he got only $5.

Nevertheless many commissioners signed warrants reluctantly. Some refused. Others were known to tip off Underground operators that warrants had been issued and to warn them to get their charges out of town at once.

Few Northern law officers enforced the act with any show of enthusiasm. Sometimes they looked the other way when a fugitive was escaping. They may have had no use for abolitionists, but they had respect for personal rights and it went against their grain to see human beings treated merely as property.

A few Southerners abetted the Underground movement. But generally planters, hired slave catchers and some officials pursued the fugitives without mercy.

The abolitionists were just as determined and they had the decided advantage of knowing the lay of the land. It was easy to throw the Southern hunters off the scent.

The Underground concocted such gimmicks as this cryptic message from an agent in the South to an operative in the North: "Tomorrow you will receive two copies of 'the Irrepressible Conflict' bound in black."

That meant that two slaves were in transit. The prophetic phrase, "irrepressible conflict," meaning civil war, was coined by Senator William H. Seward in a Rochester speech in 1858.

An immediate effect of the drastic law of 1850 was to send thousands of Negroes who had found havens in the Northern states stampeding to Canada via the Underground.

This stream, added to the constant flow from the South, brought the estimated number of Negroes in Canada at the outbreak of the Civil War to 50,000.

The fugitives came into New York State mostly from Philadelphia, where the intrepid Negro, William Still, ran a busy station, via Harrisburg and Williamsport. Elmira was the focal point north of the state border. From there the trails forked. One led to the Niagara—to Buffalo, Black Rock and Lewiston; another to Rochester and other mid-Lake Ontario ports and a third swung east to Oswego by way of Ithaca or Auburn and Syracuse. Stations were from 12 to 20 miles apart.

Other routes wound into New York State from Ohio and Pittsburgh. They made the Jamestown area and Olean important stations from which the routes radiated. Always the ultimate destination was Canada. The Underground's lines had to be flexible. If there ever were any maps, none has been preserved. The whole operation was "top secret."

Most of the escapees wound up in the Canadian province of Ontario. Some flocked to the cities, principally London, Hamilton, St. Catharines, Kingston and Toronto. Others worked on farms. Some bought land.

Liberal Canada, which in the beginning had encouraged the Underground influx, became dismayed at the swelling flood of refugees and began to show some coolness to the newcomers before the Civil War ended the Underground operation.

After the war the majority of the fugitives left Canada for the States. By 1872 there were only 20,000 Negroes in the Dominion.

Exactly how many slaves escaped from bondage through the Underground is anybody's guess. Thousands of runaways stayed in the North and never tried to reach Canada. The heaviest concentration was in the Middle Western states because of their proximity to the slavery realm. To reach New York State the escapees had to cross the broad stretches of Pennsylvania.

Besides the regular Underground operatives, estimated at more than 3,000, there were a few professional "Negro stealers," mercenary adventurers with no special sympathy for the slaves or any deep dislike of slavery. They were paid by Negroes in the free states and in Canada to bring relatives and friends out of the South. The Underground had no part in this traffic, but no station master ever turned away a slave, no matter who brought him in.

Without the Fugitive Slave Law, the Underground Railroad would never have assumed its massive proportions. That "damnable law," as the abolitionists termed it, was the spark that ignited the powder keg. At that only a fragment of the Northern people took part in the enterprise. Many opposed it. Most citizens ignored it. It was a case of one "minority group" rescuing another.

The historian, Albert Bushnell Hart, summed up the Underground's place in the story of America ably:

"The Underground Railroad was a form of . . . defiance of national laws on the ground that they were unjust and oppressive. It was the unconstitutional but logical refusal of several thousand people to acknowledge that they owed any regard to slavery or were bound to look on fleeing bondmen as the property of the slave holders, no matter how the laws read.

"It was also a practical means of bringing anti-slavery principles to the attention of the lukewarm or pro-slavery people in free states, and of convincing the South that the abolitionist movement was sincere and effective.

"Above all the Underground Railroad was the opportunity for the bold and the adventurous. . . . It was one of the forces that brought on the Civil War and that doomed slavery."

The Underground bred some heroic figures and some villains—as we shall see.

Chapter 5

A Female "Moses"

"On my Underground Railroad I nebber run de train off de track and I nebber lost a passenger."

That was the proud and truthful boast of Harriet Tubman, who personally led out of bondage more than 300 of her people. To them she was their "Moses," another Joan of Arc. After the Civil War came, the "one-woman Underground" served as a nurse and spy for the Union army and even led soldiers into battle.

John Brown always addressed her as "General Tubman." Thomas Higginson, the patrician Boston abolitionist called her "the greatest heroine of her age." Intellectuals shared the platform with this former slave who had never learned to read or write. Books have been written about her life.

For more than 50 of her 92 years she called Auburn home. The Finger Lakes city honors her memory with a tablet imbedded in the front wall of the Cayuga County Court House. Her old home on the outskirts of the town where she aided so many of her race is to them a national shrine.

Harriet Tubman did not look like a Joan of Arc. She was black as a lump of coal. She was five feet tall, with the biceps of a Joe Louis. Her upper front teeth were missing. She wore a red bandana over her short kinky hair. To her people it was the plumed helmet of a Crusader. She wore threadbare clothes but under them beat the heart of a lion.

Born in a slave cabin and denied any semblance of schooling, as a girl she heard others read Bible verses and she committed them to memory. The time came when she addressed audiences in Northern cities with all the poise of a Wendell Phillips. Her simple, dramatic recital of her experiences, told in plantation idiom, made many friends for her cause.

She was not concerned with emancipation. Her objective was simply to get as many of her people out of slavery and into "the promised land."

Slave owners lost some $300,000 in human chattels through "General" Tubman's 19 raids on their plantations, mostly in Maryland. They put a price of $12,000 on her head. But she never was caught and she "nebber lost a passenger."

Harriet Tubman was born about 1820 in Dorchester County on Maryland's Eastern Shore. Her family belonged to a planter who owned so many slaves he hired some of them out to others. The girl was given the first name of her mother, Harriet, and the last name of her father, Ross. There was not a drop of white blood in her.

From childhood she encountered only cruelty, except from her parents. At the age of five, Harriet was lashed by her mistress because she was slow to grasp the details of house work and she was sent into the fields. When she was seven the girl was caught stealing a lump of sugar. She ran away and hid in a pig pen for five days before hunger forced her return—to suffer a flogging.

At 12 she was doing a man's work. Her muscles grew,

her hands became calloused and the sullen rebellion mounted in her heavy-lidded eyes. When she was in her teens, she refused to help an overseer tie up a balky slave. The white man threw an iron weight at her. It struck her on the head and for months her life hung by a thread. After she recovered, she was subject to spells of stupor and carried a scar on her head to the grave.

So it was little wonder that hatred of slavery became a passion with her. She began to dream of freedom when through the "grapevine" came tales of a mysterious "Underground" which carried slaves to free soil.

When she was 25, Harriet married John Tubman, an easy-going free Negro, who had no sympathy with her craving for freedom. After five years of unhappy married life, she made her first escape attempt. She induced her three brothers to join her but after a few miles they became scared and dragged her back with them to the plantation. Now she faced the threat of being "sold South."

She determined to escape alone. A white neighbor woman gave her a paper on which was written two names and told the girl how to reach the first house named. There a farmer looked at the note, tucked Harriet into his wagon, threw a sack over and drove her to the next station. From station to station she traveled by night until finally she "crossed the line" into Pennsylvania.

In Philadelphia she obtained work as a domestic and there met William Sill, a free Negro and "chief brakeman" on the Underground. Sill sent countless fugitives over the invisible railway. Harriet familiarized herself with the workings of the Underground, saved her money and prepared to go South and bring out members of her family.

She met her sister and two children in Baltimore where they had been taken by others and she escorted them to free soil. That was the most simple of her many raids on the slave country.

In 1851 she went back to the Eastern Shore, hoping to persuade her husband to escape. She found he had re-married. She gathered a band of other slaves and piloted them to Philadelphia. Once she led out 11, including a brother and his wife. Their escape route led through Rochester on the way to the Canadian haven, St. Catharines.

She had a fellow-conspirator write a code letter telling her people of her approach. It read: "Tell my brothers to be always watching unto prayer and when the good ship of Zion comes along to be ready to step aboard."

The Biblical wording fooled postal authorities who intercepted such messages. They questioned the writer who declared he did not understand what it meant himself.

From 1851 to 1857 Harriet made St. Catharines her base, from which she made 11 raids on Maryland and neighboring states. She worked at intervals in the Canadian city to finance her forays.

Harriet Tubman planned her campaigns like a military chief of staff. She enforced iron discipline. She revealed few of her plans and her people trusted her implicitly. She developed many stratagems, including a system of passes and codes.

The "female Moses" sometimes dressed her male fugitives as women and the women as men. More than once slaves escaped in the carriages of their owners. They also were hidden in wagons and covered with produce.

"Keep moving" was Harriet's constant cry. She urged her charges on in spite of fatigue and sickness. When one man in a group of 25 panicked and was about to run back to

Portrait of Harriet Tubman

The Tubman Home in Auburn

the plantation, Harriet shoved a revolver into his ribs and told him to keep moving or be shot. He kept moving.

With only the North Star as her guide, she would lead her "army" over the freedom road, singing

I'll meet you in the morning,
Safe in the promised land;
On the other side of Jordan,
Bound for the promised land.

She would improvise new words for old plantation tunes. In her old age she would sometimes repeat the chant the weary fugitives sang as they plodded northward:

There's cider in the cellar,
And the black folks they'll have some;
Must be now the kingdom coming,
And the year of jubilum.

When bawling children threatened to betray a party on entering a town, Harriet would dose the youngsters with paregoric and tuck them in a huge ticking bag she always carried.

Always she lived dangerously. Often she escaped capture by minutes. Once she scented danger on a main road, left it and plunged into a stream up to her armpits. Her band followed without a murmur.

Again, when the enemy closed in on her in a railway station, she calmly pretended to be reading a book. That fooled her pursuers. One of them said, "This can't be the Tubman woman. The poster says she can't read or write." At another time friends found her sound asleep under one of those big posters which advertised a reward for her capture.

She was a consummate actress. When cornered, she could

transform herself in a twinkling into a feeble, tottering old woman. In 1859, while Maryland slave holders were holding a state convention to plan action against her, she led a raid on an adjoining town.

A line of the Underground ran through Auburn, where lived a number of Quakers and other abolitionists and which housed several secret hiding places for fugitive slaves. In the mid 1850s Harriet first met Auburn's leading citizen, former Gov. William H. Seward, then a leader of the anti-slavery forces in the Senate. They became friends.

In 1857 Harriet decided to settle in Auburn although until after the war she was to spend only brief intervals there. Seward provided her with a home, a two-story brick house which still stands at the end of South Street on the outskirts of the city. Later he sold it to her for a nominal sum. That action was illegal and, had it been publicized at the time, would have injured Seward's Presidential ambitions. Harriet brought to the South Street home her aged parents whom she had taken out of slave territory and also used it as an Underground station.

Frances Seward did not have to be as circumspect about openly espousing the Abolitionist cause as did her politically ambitious husband. After Harriet had taken her favorite niece, Margaret Stewart, out of Maryland, she brought the girl to the Seward mansion. There Margaret became virtually a member of the household and was taught manners and the other things a lady should know. When Aunt Harriet visited Auburn, Margaret would meet the Underground conductor in the Seward carriage.

"General" Tubman was deeply involved in John Brown's mad schemes and only illness prevented her from joining him in the Harper's Ferry fiasco. Harriet venerated the memory of "the Old Man," as she called Brown. To her he was a true liberator. Lincoln she disdained for his delay in freeing the Negroes.

The outbreak of the Civil War found Harriet in Canada. She hurried to the border and induced many slaves to escape to the Union lines. After the Federals took Port Royal, S.C. in 1862, she nursed sick Negroes there and helped establish a hospital for them.

Soon she reported to General Hunter as an espionage agent. She was given command of a party of scouts and river pilots who spied on the enemy and turned in some valuable information.

In July, 1863, the "General" took the field. Carrying rifle, haversack and first aid satchel, and wearing bloomers and a blue coat, she guided 300 Negro soldiers into enemy country along the Comcahee River in South Carolina. Her "division" burned supplies and buildings and liberated nearly 800 slaves. At that time Harriet met a powerfully-built soldier named Nelson Davis, ten years her junior. She married him in Auburn in 1869 in Central Church with the Sewards and other socialites attending, along with many Negroes.

In May 1864 while she was home on leave, Harriet was taken ill and neighbors brought her delicacies. After her recovery she joined the nursing corps and upon the recommendation of Secretary of State Seward, was made matron of the Army Hospital at Fortress Monroe, Va. When she tried to collect for her services, even the powerful Secretary couldn't help.

Homeward bound from the war, she encountered the same brutality she had known as a young slave. She got on the wrong train by mistake. The conductor ordered her to get off. When she protested that she was entitled to the same treatment as white soldiers, he tried to remove her by force. She put up a fight and it took the conductor and three other men to throw her into a baggage car. She was injured in the fracas.

Bruised and broke, Harriet Tubman came home. She found her work for her people was far from completed. The aged and destitute of her race swarmed to her door. She turned none away. She fed and nursed them, often going hungry herself. Rich Auburn folk donated food and clothing.

Mrs. Sarah Bradford of Geneva wrote a book, *The Life and Times of Harriet Tubman,* and turned over the proceeds, $1,200 to the onetime conductor of the Underground. The money went to help the freedmen in the South and the refugees at home.

Always in her mind was a grand objective—a haven at Auburn for the aged and indigent of her people. She peddled from house to house the produce she and her "guests" raised in her garden. Every cent she could spare went into the fund for the home.

After her husband died in 1888 she got her first government check as the widow of a war veteran. That meant $8 a month for the fund. In the late 1890s prominent Auburnians pushed a bill through Congress allowing her $20 a month for the rest of her life. A South Carolina Congressman fought the measure all the way.

In 1896 she took a bold step. At an auction she bid in for $1,450 the 25-acre plot adjoining her home, which she mortgaged as part of the transaction. White and Negro friends helped her project along. In 1903 she deeded the property to the African Methodist Episcopal Zion Church.

Finally in 1908 her dream came true. The home for the aged was opened in two buildings already on the plot, one of frame, the other of brick. As long as she lived the home sheltered from 12 to 15 persons at a time.

In the twilight of her long life Harriet Tubman became a living legend. She had notable visitors, among them Booker T. Washington, the Negro educator. Queen Victoria sent her a Diamond Jubilee medal and invited her to England. Writers for newspapers and magazines interviewed the old lady. A new generation read the story of her heroism and devotion to her people.

On May 10, 1913 the 92-year-old woman called two ministers and a few friends to her bedside. After the ministers had prayed over her, she asked the others to strike up a song. With the last strains of "Swing Low, Sweet Chariot," Harriet Tubman "went home." The Grand Army of the Republic buried their wartime comrade with military honors.

When the memorial tablet to the "Moses of her people," erected by the community at the Court House, was dedicated, Auburn's mayor proclaimed the day, June 12, 1914, a civic holiday. Booker T. Washington came again to Auburn to lead the eulogies in which leading white citizens joined. In 1944 during World War II the United States launched a Liberty Ship and christened it the Harriet Tubman.

Deprived of her guiding hand and executive ability, the home for the aged which she had founded lasted only a few years after her death. The buildings fell into disrepair and the brick structure was razed. The frame house in which Mrs. Tubman died, rotted away until the city ordered it demolished in 1944.

Then Bishop William J. Wallis of the A.M.E. Zion Church organized a drive for its restoration and $30,000 was raised. On April 13, 1953 the Harriet Tubman Home, rebuilt and modernized, was dedicated under the auspices of the church.

The year before the Rev. Arthur E. May and his wife, Margaret, came to take care of the property. May is still its director and Mrs. May is executive secretary of the church women's foreign missionary society which has its headquarters there. May found the plot grown up to weeds and has landscaped the grounds around the house. But much remains to be done.

Church groups make pilgrimages to the place which is a shrine to many of Harriet's people. The names of visitors from many states and some foreign lands are on the guest book. Students from upstate colleges come to engage in research. The room in which Harriet died has been restored. On the wall is an oil painting of the heroine of the Underground, wearing her bandana.

The brick house next door where Harriet lived so long and where she first sheltered her people, passed out of the hands of her family and now is a private residence. It is a link with the Underground and a historic one.

The church still is determined to fulfil Harriet Tubman's dream and build a home for the aged on the 25-acre site, which also would serve as a center for summer conferences.

Her people remember her incessant command to the fugitives she led out of bondage so long ago. It was "Keep Moving."

Chapter 6

Frederick the Great

As a young slave in Maryland, Frederick Bailey had known of the Underground Railroad but when the time came for him to escape from bondage, he rode northward on a regular passenger train, not on the shadowy line which had no rails or locomotives.

The handsome, well-built 21-year-old mulatto with the leonine head little dreamed then that one day he would be one of the masterminds of "Operation Underground."

His first direct contact with the Underground came in 1838 when on his arrival in New York in a borrowed Navy uniform, friendless and nearly penniless, he was sheltered by its agents. They found work for him in New England where Fred Bailey was given a new and more romantic name, borrowed from Scott's *Lady of the Lake*.

His new name was Frederick Douglass and under that name he became the foremost Negro of his time, a magnetic orator, a gifted editor-writer and a consummate politician.

For a quarter of a century Rochester was his home base. As stationmaster of the Underground in the lakeside city, he directed the escape of hundreds of fugitive slaves to Canada, in defiance of the law. At the same time he was publishing an abolitionist journal and lecturing on two continents. Douglass came to know some of the great ones of his time.

Douglass was to engineer many a masterful escape plan but none was more ingenious than his own break for freedom. One September day in 1838 he jumped aboard a northbound train as it was pulling out of Baltimore. He was wearing a United States Navy uniform, borrowed from a free Negro who had been a sailor. He also had his sailor friend's "protection paper." It was embossed with the gold seal of the Union and the conductor gave the paper only a cursory glance.

So Fred Bailey stepped off the train in New York, on free soil. It was the turning point of his life.

Born on a plantation in Talbot County on Maryland's Eastern Shore around February, 1817 (he never knew his exact birth date) he had only vague memories of his mother who was sold and went away when he was very young. He never knew the name of his white father. He lived with his grandparents and he took their name, Bailey.

His early years were happy ones, spent in "The Big House," where he was well treated and later in Baltimore, where his kindly master and mistress taught him to read and write.

Sent to the plantation of his master's brother, he came to know brutality and injustice. When he protested against the whipping of other slaves and was caught teaching some of them to read and write, he got the reputation of being "an uppity nigger." He was turned over to an overseer to be "broken in." That bully beat and half starved him. He never forgot those experiences.

On his return to his master's home in Baltimore, his fortunes improved. He worked as a calker in a shipyard and was allowed to keep a small part of his pay. He saved every cent he could, because he was determined to be free.

He began attending meetings of a free Negro society and at one of them made his first speech, a clumsy but effective plea against the proposed colonization of Negroes in Africa. And there he met and fell in love with Anna Murray, born free.

In New York a Negro, David Ruggles, and other agents of the Underground sheltered the runaway and arranged for Anna to join him. After their marriage, they went to New Bedford, Mass., where Frederick got work in the shipyards. He was taken under the wing of Nathan Johnson, a free Negro, who gave him his new name, Frederick Douglass.

He began reading William Lloyd Garrison's uncompromising abolitionist paper, the *Liberator*. He attended anti-slavery lectures, listened, studied and began speaking at meetings of the Negro community.

Douglass developed poise and skill as a speaker and attracted the attention of white abolitionists. In 1841 he was persuaded to speak at an all-white gathering for the first time. When he demurred, a friend, William Coffin, an Underground leader, told him:

"Just tell your story, Frederick, as you have told it so many times to me."

With simple, moving eloquence Frederick told his story. His audience was impressed. So was Garrison, who was on the platform. Soon Douglass was an agent and lecturer for the Massachusetts Anti-Slavery Society. He lectured in friendly New England and Upstate New York.

When he invaded the Middle West, he found the crusader's path a thorny one. In some towns he was mobbed, beaten, pelted with rotten fruit and hissed. He encountered

"Jim Crowism" in restaurants, hotels and trains along the way.

But he kept on. As he broadened his education through study and association with intellectuals, he injected the political and economic aspects of the slavery issue into his speeches. Actually his lot had been easier than that of most slaves, but none could speak so eloquently as he.

In 1845 he published the first of his three autobiographies, *Narrative of the Life of Frederick Douglass*. It was a national sensation. Feeling against him ran so high in the South that he boarded ship for England to avoid being taken back in bondage.

During his 23 months in the British Isles, he made some valuable contacts and aroused sympathy among statesmen and working people. He formed a friendship with two well-to-do English sisters, Julia and Eliza Griffis, who were to play important roles in his later career. And he came home, a free man. The Women's Anti-Slavery Society of Britain had purchased his freedom.

Along with a new beard, he came home with $2,300, which had been raised for his cause by English friends. Douglass decided to start an abolition paper of his own, against the wishes of the Boston abolitionists who did not see the need of another anti-slavery organ and who believed Douglass was more effective as a speaker than as a writer.

Douglass was not deterred from his plan but decided to launch his journalistic venture outside of New England. He chose Rochester because of its liberal attitude and its location midway between New England and the West. Nothing in his memoirs indicates that Rochester's position as a lake port or that the Underground entered into his calculations then.

In December, 1847, Douglass's four-page weekly, the

North Star, made its bow. There is a tradition the paper was born in the African Methodist Zion Church in Rochester's Favor Street. For years the journal, later renamed the *Frederick Douglass Paper,* was printed in an office at the Four Corners on the present site of the Wilder Building.

The Griffis sisters came from England to help Douglass with his paper and to live in the editor's home at 4 (now 297) Alexander St. Disenchanted with the Rochester weather, Eliza returned to England but Julia stayed on for several years. Her presence in the Douglass household caused some gossip, and Garrison, who had broken with Douglass over matters of policy, printed a sly innuendo in his journal.

The abolitionist camp was split, with the Garrisonians adopting a course of "moral suasion," while Douglass joined the forces led by Gerrit Smith who advocated direct political action.

Enactment of the drastic Fugitive Slave Law in 1850 intensified the activities of the Underground in and around Rochester and Douglass emerged as the chief conductor and master of the key Rochester station. It is estimated that under his direction a total of nearly 500 slaves passed through the city on their way to Canada via lake boats. Most of them found a haven in St. Catharines.

Douglass deplored the lack of secrecy manifested in Western operations of the Underground in his second book, *My Bondage and My Freedom,* published in 1855. He wrote:

"I have never approved of the very public manner in which some of our Western friends have conducted what they call the Underground Railroad, but, which I think by their open declarations, has been made most emphatically 'the Upper-ground Railroad.'

"Its stations seem better known to the slaveholders than to the slaves. I honor these good men and women for their noble devotion in willingly subjecting themselves to persecution, by openly avowing their participation in the escape of slaves. Nevertheless the good resulting from such avowals is of very questionable character.

"We owe something to the slaves, south of Mason's and Dixon's Line, as well as those to the north of it, and in discharging this duty of aiding the latter on their way to freedom, we should be careful to do nothing to hinder the former in making their escape to slavery."

In the Rochester sector no such hindrance was evident.

Douglass hid hundreds of slaves in his printing office and in his home in the heyday of the Underground. Many a night he would hear a light tap at the door of his house on Alexander Street west of East Avenue—and his later residence on South Avenue near the present Highland Park. He would find frightened black faces at the door and none was ever turned away.

He wrote that "on one occasion I had at least 11 fugitives at the same time under my roof—until I could collect sufficient money to get them to Canada. It was the largest number at any one time and I had some difficulty in providing so many food and shelter. But they were content with very plain food and a strip of carpet on the floor for a bed or a place in the straw of the hayloft."

One of his principal Rochester aides in raising funds for the Underground was J. P. Morris. He also called on friends in England for frequent assistance.

The Rochester station master had many a dramatic

experience in keeping the runaways out of the hands of the slave catchers.

On one occasion a prominent Democrat—and few Democrats were abolitionists—who was the law partner of the United States commissioner sought Douglass out to tip him off that papers were being prepared for the arrest of three fugitives from Maryland.

One of the hunted men was at that moment in Douglass's own home, another was sheltered on Asa Anthony's farm on the western outskirts of Rochester and the third was in the old Quaker settlement at Farmington. Swift horses went into action and before the papers could be served, the three men were safely aboard a Canada-bound ship.

Douglass had a hand in a similar episode also involving three Negroes, who stayed for months in Rochester and even attended anti-slavery meetings in Corinthian Hall. Word came to Douglass their master was in town and had a warrant for their arrest. For three days the men were hidden in various places. Then one dark night, dressed in Quaker bonnets and heavily veiled, they were driven to Charlotte in a closed carriage and put aboard a waiting boat while a marshal was looking for them.

Douglass once provided sanctuary to three other Negroes, one of them a minister named Parker, who were sought for the killing of one of their pursuers and wounding another at Parker's home in Christiana, Pa.

A large reward was out for their capture and the officers were hot on their trail. Douglass acted swiftly. He sent Julia Griffis to the river landing to arrange for their passage to Canada on a British boat. Disguising the three men in women's garb, Douglass put them in a carriage and drove them to the docks, where they climbed aboard the boat just as it was about to put out. Parker handed Douglass as a souvenir the pistol which had killed the slave hunter in Pennsylvania.

Douglass led many a weary, frightened group to Zion Church where they were hidden in the pews and basement until they could be spirited off to freedom.

He worked closely with the indomitable Harriet Tubman, "the female Moses" of her people, who directed so many slaves along the liberty road. And Douglass had many allies in Rochester who willingly gave refuge to the fugitives.

One of Douglass's aides was William S. Falls, who was the foreman of the job room of the *Daily Democrat,* which was on another floor of the building which housed Douglass's printing office. In off hours Falls would secrete fugitive slaves behind the presses of his job room. He also solicited funds for the runaways in the old Reynolds Arcade and in other downtown places. Falls said "the poor creatures were often penniless." Few of the citizens he approached turned him down.

Douglass was a busy man, getting out his paper and making many speeches, besides directing the traffic on the Underground through one of its key stations. The railroad had no more successful station master, for never was a fugitive slave caught in Rochester while he ran the line.

Among the many abolitionists of Douglass' acquaintance was a fiery old man named John Brown. When the two men met in Springfield, Mass., where Brown was a wool dealer long before the old fanatic went on the rampage in "bleeding Kansas," he unfolded to Douglass a plan for freeing many slaves. He proposed to mass small bands of escaped slaves in the mountains near the border and raid plantations for more recruits. It was not a large-scale operation and Douglass thought well of it.

He kept in touch with Brown and in 1858 the latter, using the name, Nelson Hawkins, visited Douglass and told of a new and grandiose scheme. It involved seizure of the United States Arsenal at Harper's Ferry, Va. and the insurrection of thousands of slaves. The practical Douglass sensed that such a plan could not suceed and as the two men walked Rochester's southern hills, he tried in vain to dissuade Brown from his fantastic course.

Three weeks before the date set for the Harper's Ferry raid Brown called Douglass to a conference at Chambersburg, Pa. The pair met in a quarry in the hills. Brown implored Douglass to join in the raid. Douglass refused.

He had taken with him a giant Negro, Shields "Emperor" Green. When it came time to leave, Green said quietly, "I stay with the old man." He stayed and was captured with the survivors of Brown's band when the Federal troops put down the insurrection at the arsenal.

Douglass was speaking in Philadelphia when he learned of the fiasco. In his home in Rochester were incriminating letters from John Brown. He telegraphed his son, Lewis, to secrete the papers.

Douglass was deeply involved and for the second time fled the country. He was in Canada when United States marshals arrived in Rochester with a Virginia warrant for his arrest. From Canada he sailed for England. Five months later he was called home by the death of a daughter. He was not arrested on his return.

Douglass had hoped that his friend, William H. Seward, would be the Republican standard bearer in 1860 but after Abraham Lincoln won the nomination, he took the stump for the gaunt Illinois politician.

The outbreak of the Civil War removed the need for any Underground Railroad or any anti-slavery journals. The issue was to be settled on the battlefield. Douglass turned to campaigning for the enlistment of Negroes as regular soldiers in the Union army and for emancipation of the slaves.

Lincoln took his time in taking these steps and Douglass was irked, but he kept on good terms with the White House. When finally the blue ranks were opened to Negroes, he issued his famous call, "Men of Color, To Arms." He helped recruit two Negro regiments and saw two of his sons march off to war.

After the Northern victory he joined the successful battle for adoption of the 14th Amendment granting the Negro equal citizenship. That had been the supreme goal of his long crusade.

Fire destroyed the Douglass home in Rochester in 1872 and the family moved to Washington. As the spokesman for thousands of newly enfranchised Negroes, Douglass was a political power and Republican Presidents showered offices on him. He was successively United States marshal and recorder of deeds for the District of Columbia and minister to Haiti.

Anna, the wife of his youth, died in 1884. Two years later the 67-year-old Negro leader married a white woman 20 years his junior. Helen Pitts had been his secretary. As a young child she had first seen Douglass when he visited her abolitionist father, Gideon Pitts, in their Honeoye home.

The marriage caused much commotion in Washington, as well as in Rochester and Honeoye. Douglass shrugged it off with the comment: "My first wife was the color of my mother. My second wife is the color of my father."

Death came to Frederick Douglass in Washington in 1895. He came back to Rochester—to lie in state in City Hall and to be eulogized by suffrage leader Susan B. Anthony at a public service in Central Presbyterian Church. His widow died in 1903 and is buried beside her husband in Rochester's Mount Hope Cemetery.

On June 9, 1899, thousands gathered in the triangle at St. Paul Street and Clinton Avenue North near Rochester's New York Central Station for the dedication of a life-size bronze statue of Frederick Douglass. The orator of the day was Theodore Roosevelt, then Governor of New York.

After 42 years downtown, the monument was moved to an eminence overlooking the Highland Park Bowl. There, his arms outstretched as if pleading his people's cause, the onetime station master of the Underground stands—near his old home and among the rolling hills where long ago he and old John Brown walked and talked.

Chapter 7

One-Man Underground

When Calvin Fairbank was 12 years old, he spent a night with his parents in the Allegany County home of a Negro couple who had escaped from slavery.

The stories the old couple told of 30 years of suffering and cruelty in bondage haunted the boy and instilled in him a hatred of slavery that amounted almost to an obsession.

Calvin Fairbank, born in 1816 in a log cabin in the Town of Pike, was probably the most daring of the abolitionists and is now one of the most forgotten. He suffered far more for the cause than did William Lloyd Garrison, Wendell Phillips and many another crusader with pen and tongue.

For guiding some 50 Negroes to free soil at different times as a lone wolf operator along the Ohio River and for his part in the sensational auction of a lovely slave girl, he spent 17 years in Kentucky prisons. He was the most hated "nigger stealer" in the Blue Grass State.

Fairbank's first rescue, a minor exploit, was in 1837. He had left Olean on the Allegany on a river raft and was on the Ohio River close to the Virginia side when he spied a Negro on the shore. He asked the slave if he would like to be free. The Negro would, and he jumped aboard the raft which Fairbank poled to shore. The fugitive was landed safely on free Ohio ground and young Calvin was launched on his new career.

On that same trip Fairbank took 15 other slaves, including a family of seven, across the river and delivered them to agents of the Underground. The next year he helped 12 more Negroes to freedom, was pursued by slaveholders but managed to reach sanctuary in Logansburg, Ind.

In 1843, still courting trouble, Fairbank was in Lexington, Ky., where he heard about a lovely slave girl being held at the local jail pending her sale at auction. She was a gifted musician and as white as any Southern belle. Her mistress was jealous of her beauty and talents and wanted her out of the way.

Fairbank visited the girl in her cell and promised to help her gain her freedom. He went to Cincinnati and raised a fund of more than $2,000 to buy her. Among the donors to the fund were Salmon P. Chase, who was to become Lincoln's Secretary of the Treasury, and Nicholas Longworth, Sr.

When the girl was put on the block in Lexington, the bidding, at first spirited, narrowed to Fairbank and a Creole dandy from New Orleans, who eyed the slave's charms greedily. When Fairbank upped his bid to $1,400, the Creole hesitated.

Then the auctioneer stripped the girl before the crowd, garment by garment, shouting, "Here's a lass fit to be mistress to a king!" There were those in the crowd who cried: "Shame!" Some women hastily departed. In later years Fairbank said that had he been armed, he would have shot that auctioneer on the spot.

After Fairbank raised his bid to $1,485, the other man

quit. The girl was given her immediate freedom and in a few years married a prominent Cincinnati white man.

That incident occurred while Fairbank was studying for the ministry in Oberlin College. After his graduation in 1844, with the help of a fellow teacher, a Miss Webster of Massachusetts, he got a Negro family of three out of Lexington and across the river to Ohio. On their return to Lexington, both were arrested. Miss Webster was convicted, but was pardoned by the Governor. Fairbank pleaded guilty and was sentenced to 15 years in Frankfort prison.

Northern friends petitioned for his pardon. His aged father went to Kentucky to intercede with the Governor, died of the cholera and was buried in Kentucky. After Calvin Fairbank had served five years of his sentence, he got a pardon from Governor John J. Crittenden, a former attorney-general of the United States.

Then he embarked on a lecture tour and became closely associated with Garrison, Phillips and other Northern Abolitionists. His recital of his experiences moved his audiences.

But Kentucky had not forgotten nor forgiven "the nigger stealer."

In the Fall of 1851 Fairbank went South to bring home the body of his father. While in Indiana he could not resist helping a fugitive slave. Unfriendly Indiana authorities surrendered him to a Kentucky sheriff and again he faced a biased court. Fairbank conducted his own defense ably but was sentenced to 15 years in Frankfort prison—for the second time.

An attempt to break jail during his trial did not help his case. It merely put him in irons until after he was convicted. In prison he was assigned the toughest manual labor and when he was unable to stand any more, he was flogged by a keeper with a rawhide soaked in water.

Fairbank related in after years that during his term he suffered 3,500 lashes on his bare back, 230 in one day. Only his splendid physique and iron will kept him alive.

During the Civil War he was thrice visited by Confederate soldiers who wanted to take him out of his cell and hang him. Twice a friendly keeper hid him and the third time Fairbank grabbed an axe and dared the Rebels to take him. His courage won their admiration and he was spared.

When he entered prison, he weighed 180 pounds. Within a year he was down to 117 pounds.

On April 16, 1864, after 12 years in prison, he was freed by the Governor of Kentucky at the personal request of President Lincoln.

Never during the rest of his days, could he hear the poignant strains of "My Old Kentucky Home" without wincing.

Before his second period of confinement, he had become engaged to a Massachusetts girl. When he offered to release her from the engagement, she said she would wait for him until he was free. She left her home to teach in Oxford, Ohio, to be nearer her betrothed. She sent him gifts, wrote him daily and strove to obtain a pardon. A few days after his release, they were married.

The story of Fairbank's martyrdom and its romantic finale was well publicized and the couple were given ovations when they visited Washington and other cities. Fairbank preached at services in Washington, attended by President Lincoln and his family and other dignitaries.

For several years after the war he conducted missions in

Richmond and New York before moving to Massachusetts where his faithful wife, Minanda, died in 1876.

Then he returned to Allegany County and settled in Angelica near the scenes of his boyhood. He remarried, received an annuity from a society organized for that sole purpose and wrote a popular book, *How the Way Was Prepared*.

Even when he was old and gray and his once stalwart frame was stooped, he worked hours in his garden. His last years were serene—in contrast to his stormy, tortured youth.

He died in 1898 and he sleeps in the Until the Dawn Cemetery at Angelica. A former Negro slave who lived in the town wept when the Rev. Calvin Fairbank was lowered into the grave.

Chapter 8

Tribune of the People

One of the mainstays of the Underground Railroad in Rochester was William Clough Bloss. He was a champion of many other unpopular causes and his remarkable career as a reformer has been singularly unsung.

His home on lower East Avenue, the present site of the Cutler Building, housed many a fugitive slave. He never turned a runaway away from his door.

His son, the late Joseph B. Bloss, recalled that when he was a young boy, his father led him to the woodshed of the East Avenue house where an escaped Negress was hiding. William Bloss bade his son place his fingers in the deep welts a slaver's lash had left on the woman's back. Then in tones his son never forgot, the pioneer abolitionist said:

"I am subject to a fine of $1,000 and imprisonment for six months for giving this woman a crust of bread, a cup of water, for not arresting her or in any way aiding her escape. Yet I shall disobey this law and when there is another like it, you shall also disobey it."

A native of Massachusetts, he had taught school in Maryland and in North Carolina. What he saw there instilled in him an abhorrence of human bondage.

In 1825 he opened a tavern on the banks of the newly-dug Erie Canal in the port of Brighton. After a prosperous year, he became disgusted with the business and joined the temperance forces. In the presence of others in the movement, he dumped into the canal his entire stock of spirits, worth hundreds of dollars, and closed the tavern.

The rest of his life he was an uncompromising fighter in many reform camps. Generally he was years in advance of his times.

In 1834 Bloss was publishing in Rochester an anti-slavery paper, *The Rights of Man,* 13 years before Frederick Douglass began printing his *North Star.*

In 1838 when Susan B. Anthony was teaching her first school, not interested in equal rights, Bloss was advocating the ballot for women.

In 1845 while a member of the Assembly, he proposed an amendment to the state constitution to give Negroes the right to vote. During a communion service in Albany, he crossed the "Jim Crow" line and leaving his seat among the whites, he partook of the Sacrament with the segregated Negroes in a corner of the church. Bloss was not re-elected to the Legislature.

In 1856 he gave to a fund to provide a Bible and a rifle to every settler bound for "bleeding Kansas," then a battleground between Free Soil and pro-slavery forces.

That same year as a supporter of Fremont, the first Republican Presidential candidate, he originated and circulated during the campaign a map showing the area and aggressions of the slave power. It was barred from the mails in the South.

For years he was a self-appointed, unpaid chaplain at the County Jail. A century before Alcoholics Anonymous was conceived, he made his home a haven for inebriates struggling to free themselves from the drink habit.

William Clough Bloss sleeps in the old Brighton Cemetery beside the abandoned bed of the old Clinton Ditch into which years ago he had dumped his stock of liquor. On one side of a massive granite monument under a bronze medallion of a lined, bearded face is a tablet on which is inscribed his name, the date of his birth, Jan. 19, 1795, and that of his death, April 18, 1863, and these words:

A Tribune of the People

William Bloss lived long enough to rejoice in the issuing of the Emancipation Proclamation by Abraham Lincoln.

Chapter 9

From Flour City to Freedom

Because it was a port on Lake Ontario and because it was the home of Frederick Douglass, master of a busy Underground station, Rochester was a key center on the rail-less railroad.

Although the Flour City was reputed to be a hotbed of the anti-slavery movement, its abolitionists were a mere handful in the 1850s in a city of some 40,000.

Still it is estimated that an average of 150 slaves each year of that decade passed through Rochester via the Underground. Many hands must have joined in keeping the tide of fugitives flowing to Canada, the land of freedom.

The Underground Railroad funneled runaway slaves into Rochester over several routes. A favorite trail led from Canandaigua via Mendon and the present Clover Street. Others came from Pittsford and many traveled the Henrietta Road from East Avon and other points.

The fugitives were taken to the Niagara Frontier and to Canada by lake boats flying the British flag which docked at the old steamboat landing on the west side of the Genesee River at the foot of the now non-existent Buell Avenue near the present Driving Park Bridge and from the port of Charlotte.

Abolitionists were active in Rochester in the 1820s, although it was 1838 before an Anti-Slavery Society was organized, with the Quaker teacher, Lindley Mott Moore, as its first president.

Later Julia Griffis, Douglass's English ally and benefactress, formed a woman's unit. Meetings of both groups were held in the Unitarian Church and in Corinthian Hall. The American Anti-Slavery Association convened here in 1852.

Despite the zeal of the abolitionists, the general public was indifferent toward the movement. Local political leaders dodged the issue by dismissing slavery as the South's internal problem. Conservatives and business men, some of whom had dealings with Southerners, shunned the abolitionists.

The press was on the whole apathetic. Among the religious denominations, the Quakers, Unitarians, Wesleyans and Congregationalists were most active in the movement.

It was the abolitionists' proud claim that while Douglass was station master in the Flour City, not a fugitive slave was recaptured in Rochester.

But in 1823, long before Douglass's advent, a Negro woman named Ellen made her way from Virginia to join her husband, a barber, in Rochester. She was tracked down and taken before Judge Moses Chapin who directed she be put in custody and returned to her master. At the doors of the Court House nearly a score of her Negro friends overpowered the law officers and carried her off.

The officers obtained reinforcements and took her from her rescuers. Ellen was put aboard a boat at Buffalo, bound for Virginia. Aboard ship she cut her throat rather than return to servitude and be separated from her husband and nine-months-old baby.

In 1832 another fugitive Negress was seized at the

Clinton House on Exchange Street. An attempt to rescue her failed, but her Negro friends followed the woman and her master to Palmyra and there liberated her.

These incidents are related in the autobiography of the Rev. Thomas James who was born in slavery in New York State. He came to Rochester in 1823 and learned to read and write in a Negro school. He organized a school for Negro children and began preaching.

In 1830 he led in the building of a small meeting house at Spring and Favor Streets, which was replaced by the African Zion Church. In 1856 James returned from New England to become pastor of the Rochester Methodist church. That building housed runaway slaves before and during his pastorate.

During the Civil War he worked with Negro prisoners and refugees for the Union army in Louisville and after the conflict was a missionary to his people in several states. This remarkable man died in 1891 at the age of 87.

A well-authenticated Underground station was the home of Druggist Isaac Post and his Quaker wife, Amy, on the west side of Sophia Street (now North Plymouth). That was a busy outpost on the freedom road after 1836 until the Civil War.

Once as many as 16 slaves were hidden there, some for a few hours, others for several days. Amy Post told how "many a time I have gone out to the barn after dark with a basket of food and frightened men crept out of the hay to take it."

The Post home, which was razed years ago, for three decades was a meeting place for the advocates of abolition, temperance, woman's rights and Spiritualism.

Amy Post had a restless, far-ranging mind. She was the first to urge the Fox sisters, founders of modern Spiritualism, to charge fees for their seances. She and her husband were convinced of the sincerity of the sisters, who in later years confessed they had faked the "rappings" that had made them famous in their youth.

When Douglass first came to Rochester to speak, only five years away from slavery and a virtual unknown, he was entertained by the Posts and remained their lifelong friend.

Bookseller Samuel D. Porter made no secret of his alliance with the Underground movement. He hid slaves in the barn behind his home on South Fitzhugh Street, just north of the old Fitzhugh Apartments. Once a family of five Negroes was secreted in hay in the Porter barn and escaped detection when the slave catchers came.

Porter, a man of cultivated tastes, was a member of the Pundit Club, made up of Rochester intellectuals. Besides being the first secretary of the city's Anti-Slavery Society, he was several times the candidate of the Liberty Party for mayor. In 1844 he received 109 votes out of 3,200 ballots cast. That was his best run. For many years he was the only resident of the patrician Third Ward to vote the Liberty Party ticket.

He was a close friend of Douglass and urged the Negro leader to flee the country after the John Brown fiasco at Harper's Ferry. When 10-year old Anne Douglass died in 1860 and her parents had no burial plot, Samuel Porter had the child buried in his family's lot in Mount Hope Cemetery. He never ceased to work for the welfare of the Negro people until he died in 1881.

Another unquestioned Underground station was the sail loft of Edward C. Williams on Buffalo (Main) Street near the Four Corners. There slaves were hidden among the ropes and canvas.

As early as 1827 George Avery's store at 12 Buffalo St. near the Williams sail loft was a known haven for fugitives. Avery, who founded the Monroe County Bible Society with the slogan, "a Bible in every home," sold the Good Book by day and worked as an Underground agent by night.

The residence of Dr. L. C. Dolley and his physician wife, Sarah Adamson Dolley on East Avenue adjoining the William Bloss station, was commonly regarded as a hideout for escaped slaves.

Sarah Dolley, a Philadelphia Quakeress, was one of the first women licensed to practice medicine in the United States. Her husband was a professor of surgery at the short-lived Central Eclectic Medical College in Rochester, before resuming general practice.

The Dolley home was a gathering place for liberals and cultured people. Sarah Dolley founded the Women's Study Club. Imaginative writers have liked to picture the intelligentsia of Rochester sipping tea and discussing intellectual problems in the Dolley parlor while fugitive slaves cowered silently in the cellar. It just may have happened that way.

Nelson Bostwick, Douglass' neighbor on Alexander Street, was active in the movement. So presumably was Benjamin Fish, Hicksite Quaker, early miller and State Street merchant, who also was an all-around non-conformist. He was one of the founders of the Fourierist Utopian colony on Sodus Bay in the 1840s.

In front of a big square white house with green blinds and a cupola on the East Henrietta Road beside the Barge Canal in Brighton stands a county historical marker which reads:

"Warrant Homestead. Settled in 1819 by Thomas

Warrant, coppersmith and abolitionist. This home was used as a station of the Underground."

A great-granddaughter of the pioneer, Miss Cora Warrant, retired director of the Rochester Visiting Nurses Association, lives there with her mother, Mrs. Lena Warrant, now in her 100th year.

Thomas Warrant came to Rochester in 1818 from his native Yarmouth, England, by way of Canada. He had to smuggle his tools across the border because of existing laws.

After working at his coppersmith trade in Rochester for a year, he moved out into the country and built a log cabin on the site of the present homestead. The cabin, too cramped for the Warrants and their nine children, soon gave way to an "L" shaped brick house, well screened by trees.

The artisan turned farmer was a Baptist who detested slavery and hid many fugitive slaves in his barns across the road from the house or in an upper room in his home reached by a rear stairway and heated by wood-burning stoves. Never were the Warrant barns or the rear door of the house locked.

When the coast was clear he would hide his charges under hay in a wagon and drive them to stations near Lake Ontario by night.

About the time of the Civil War the house was enlarged to its present square proportions and the older brick section was covered by clapboards.

The Negro had a true friend in Thomas Warrant.

In his memoirs Douglass mentions slaves being hidden on the farm of Asa Anthony on Rapids Street (Brooks Avenue) on Rochester's western outskirts. Asa's brother, father of the immortal suffrage leader, Susan B., had a farm nearby. While he sympathized with the abolitionists, there is no record that he was an Underground operator.

His daughter, Susan, in 1857, hitherto concerned only with temperance and woman's rights, became chief Upstate agent for the American Anti-Slavery Society, working closely with Douglass and other abolitionists. There is no evidence she participated directly in the Underground.

She gave anti-slavery lectures in Rochester and other New York communities. After John Brown was executed, she organized a protest meeting which only 300 attended.

Early in January of the fateful year of 1861, she and others tried to hold an abolitionist rally in Corinthian Hall. A mob stormed the meeting and the police ended it by putting out the gas lights. The meeting was held the next day in the African Methodist Zion Church without disturbance.

Miss Anthony was trying to force the Republican Party to take a firm stand on the slavery issue. Although South Carolina had already started the secession parade, Northern leaders were pursuing a "wait and see" policy and wanted "no cranks stirring up trouble."

A neighbor and friend of the Anthony families was Rhoda De Garmo, an anti-slavery, temperance and equal rights zealot, who reputedly aided the Underground.

In his *History of the Underground Railroad,* W. H. Siebert attempts to list the Underground agents in New York and other states. On his Monroe County list appears the name of Lindley Mott Moore, the first head of the Rochester Anti-Slavery Society. Whether the scholarly Moore, who lived on Kent Street when he taught in the first Rochester High School and who later had a farm on Lake Avenue near the Lower Falls, ever harbored slaves in either residence is a moot question.

Other Rochesterians on Siebert's list, more likely to

Frederick Douglass Monument in Rochester

Warrant Homestead, a Rochester station

have been Underground conductors, are Grove S. Gilbert, distinguished portrait painter who lived on Greig Street and George H. Humphrey, a learned lawyer whose old Gothic white residence with the vertical clapboards still stands at Genesee Street and Elmdorf Avenue.

Siebert also lists as agents William and Mary Hallowell and Joseph Marsh, Douglass's next door neighbor on Alexander Street, all known abolitionists.

The stately brick residence at 1496 Clover Road, known for years as the Babcock homestead, is believed to have been an Underground station. It is as least 140 years old and was built from bricks made on the premises.

Its first occupant, Isaac Moore, was a strong abolitionist and married a kinswoman of William Clough Bloss, a pioneer in the movement. Moore's cellar at one time it is said, was stocked with choice alcoholic beverages but when he became converted to temperance, he dumped the whole supply. He held the first barn raising in Monroe County without the customary distribution of strong drinks to those who participated.

Three generations of the Babcock clan lived in the brick house, from the early 1860s until 1944. In 1895 the late A. Emerson Babcock, longtime supervisor of Brighton and a local historian of note, was installing modern plumbing in the home when a strange discovery was made.

Wooden steps leading to the cellar gave way under the weight of workmen, revealing a secret chamber, eight by 10 feet and large enough to house a dozen persons.

On the floor of that room a dozen or more chicken bones were found, indicating that runaway slaves had once been fed there. William J. Babcock Sr. of Rochester, head of the Genesee State Park Commission and son of Emerson

Babcock, recalls as a young boy seeing the "drumsticks" in the cellar.

Because of Moore's abolitionist activities, there is little doubt that the home, now owned by Edward Harris Jr., once was a station of the invisible railroad.

An enormous apartment house stands today at 1600 East Ave., the traditional site of another Underground station. In 1846 Miles Gardner, one of a family of abolitionists, lived there, and the occupant in 1853 was Henry L. Hall, who also had anti-slavery connections.

Some years ago, when a later owner, Dr. Hiram Covell, was having the old frame house remodeled, workmen discovered a curious fireplace. It appeared to be square from cellar to attic. But halfway up it shrank to a small chimney, leaving a space above it on the first floor, accessible by a trap door to the second story. Further investigation showed that the secret chamber had an outlet into the basement with vestiges of an old tunnel leading to a ravine in the rear. The ravine was filled in many years ago.

Out Clover Street beyond Mendon Ponds Park is the place where lived in Underground days Henry Quinby, listed by Siebert as a member of the undercover fraternity. The property now is owned by Dr. and Mrs. G. B. Van Alstyne. The original house has been replaced.

A handsome cobblestone house at 1191 Manitou Road in the Town of Greece near Lake Ontario has a secret cellar compartment reached by a trap door leading to a wooden stairway. It now is the residence of Arthur E. Flack. Isaac Chase, a retired New England sea captain, built the house, probably in the 1830's. His son, Isaac, Jr., lived there in the Underground time. The cellar is believed to have housed fugitive slaves, waiting for the boats to take them across the lake.

56

Legends cling to the Saxton Apartments, the big pillared structure at Plymouth Avenue South and Troup Street. In its honeycomb cellar of stone and brick is a passageway eight feet wide and 20 feet long which may have been a hiding place for fleeing slaves.

It is said that once this chamber was sealed off from the rest of the basement and could be entered only by a trap door or a tunnel. No traces of either now are visible. There are many narrow doorways and one of the several compartments, which possibly was a wine cellar, has a latticed wooden gate.

There are fantastic tales of two tunnels once connected with the basement. One supposedly led to the Genesee although what purpose it served is hard to imagine since the river, broken by waterfalls, was not a navigable stream to the lake.

Lending a spooky touch to the old house is the fact that the Fox sisters, founders of modern Spiritualism, lived there before Underground days. In the early 1850s the big building, as now, had several tenants which would knock down the story it was an Underground depot. Too many cooks in one house would spoil the broth of secrecy so necessary to UGRR operations.

Long associated with the local lore of the Underground is the "Hargous House" at 52 South Main St., Pittsford. The stately old brick building, now the St. Louis parish school, has a fascinating history.

Distiller Augustus Elliott built it in 1808 for his fiancee, a daughter of the Daniel Penfield who founded the township and village which bear his name. The story goes the girl jilted Elliott and he never lived in his mansion.

In the 1820s Judge Ashley Sampson lived there. He was a fervent abolitionist who in later years supposedly sheltered slaves in his Brooks Avenue home. He may have used the Pittsford residence for the same purpose before the Underground was in full swing.

A mysterious chamber in the basement of the Pittsford house is likely an abandoned bake oven. During the heyday of the Underground Sally Hargous, a New York socialite and no abolitionist, lived in the house the jilted distiller built.

Under Pittsford is a big natural cavern. Tradition has it a hideout for slaves, with tunnels leading to the Hargous House and other places. At any rate Pittsford would be a likely stop-over on the hush-hush railroad that ran from Canandaigua to Rochester.

The swiftly growing Town of Henrietta also figures in the tales of the Underground. David Richardson, "Uncle Dave" to the neighborhood, who weighed well over 300 pounds, lived in a farmhouse on the east side of the East Henrietta Road which is believed to have been a station. The home was torn down a few years ago to make way for the Suburban Heights real estate development.

On the edge of the village of West Henrietta stands the elegant cobblestone house that now is the home of Walter Vogel. In Underground days it was the home of Abel Post and reputedly a refuge for runaway slaves.

A newspaper clipping tells that when in recent years Frank Stanton was having the place remodeled, workmen came upon a secret basement room with iron bars on the two small windows on the grade level. Even the shutters on the windows were designed to prevent anyone from looking into the room. This has given rise to the belief held by oldtime residents that the cobblestone house was an Underground depot.

Another supposed station was the home of Deacon James

Sperry at 4747 West Henrietta Road at the corner of Lehigh Station Road. In the 1850s the deacon was a strong abolitionist, an admirer of Gerrit Smith and Garrison, and his homestead, replaced by a new house in 1896, probably housed runaway Negroes.

In the 1880s two teen-agers, sons of a minister, put out a little neighborhood paper called *The Informer.* The editors were R. J. and F. A. Strasenburgh. The former was to found a successful pharmaceutical firm bearing his name, which only recently moved to Henrietta from Rochester.

One article, headlined "Old Residenters," told of Deacon Sperry's humanitarian activities. Here are some excerpts:

"On one occasion a poor black man escaped from his cruel Master in the South and finally arrived in Henrietta on his way to Canada. Cautiously emerging from Diver's woods, he wended his way to the home of a farmer and showing cuts and stripes on his head and back caused by the lash of an overseer, he asked for assistance.

"The farmer gave him provisions and directed him that night to the residence of Deacon Sperry. 'He'll put you through all right,' said the farmer. The colored man obeyed instructions. The fugitive slave bill was then in force. . . .

"But the sturdy Deacon recognized a Higher Law than that created by an earthly tribunal—and that law bade him 'Love thy neighbor as thyself.'

"After dark the next evening the close-covered carriage of Deacon Sperry might have been seen driving toward Rochester and at 11 P.M. the noble-hearted managers of the Underground Railroad were entrusted with our colored brother who less than 24 hours thereafter found himself breathing the free air of Her Majesty's Dominion on the other side of Lake Ontario.

"Deacon Sperry was a terror to evil doers and a strong tower in defense of the downtrodden and oppressed."

It was an eloquent and moving story of Operation Underground that two teen-agers penned in Henrietta more than 80 years ago.

In Perinton there is documentary evidence that John Tallman Sr. ran an Underground station at 2187 East Whitney Road, the present home of E. P. Schermerhorn, extensively remodeled over the years. Tallman's son, John Jr., moved to Minnesota as a young man and in a paper read before the Minneapolis Historical Society, he recalled that:

"In 1859–60 a runaway slave from Georgia, his wife and half a dozen children were concealed in our house for a week on their way to Canada. They were quartered in the kitchen and provided with food . . . sufficient for several days."

He continued that "his father in the dead of night packed the family in a lumber wagon under quilts and blankets and drove them to the next station."

Still stands the massive house that Quaker abolitionist Gilbert Ramsdell built in 1816 at 173 Mason Road, north of the village of Egypt, now the farm home of Clayton Miller.

The place was so big and unusual that in the early days it was known as "Ramsdell's Castle." It has many large rooms with high ceilings. Only hand-wrought nails went into its timbers. Its high cellar walls were made of great boulders.

Gilbert Ramsdell came to Perinton from New England with his father when he was a young man. He got a job teaching school at Macedon and walked both ways. He saved his money and was able to leave the family log cabin and build a large farmhouse. After his marriage to Harriet Smith, whom he induced to join the Society of Friends, he constructed his "castle" of lumber cut on the premises.

The Ramsdell place had the reputation of being a depot of the Underground. There was no question of the Quaker deacon's sympathy for the Negroes.

But he had no tolerance for Sabbath breakers. When the young blades of Egypt began racing their horses on Mason Road on Sundays, Ramsdell put his oxen and cart squarely in their path.

An incident of Underground days was told by the late Mrs. Elizabeth M. Schilling, daughter of Joseph C. Ford who lived on the Turk Hill Road near the Steele Road intersection, in a house now gone from the scene.

Mrs. Schilling quoted a letter from her brother, Charles Wesley Ford, which related how in 1856 his mother put sandwiches for a runaway Negro on the gatepost beside the path which ran into the woods along the swampy Steele Road.

He wrote that "one morning our neighbor, Samuel Williams, had come to the door saying: 'We must help this man. We can't give him money. We can lend it to him and give him food.'" The mother's kindly deed was the result of that appeal. Years later Ford met a Negro who described the incident and the lay of the land—the swamp— the woods—the gatepost—so exactly that he was convinced that the colored man was the same one the neighborhood had befriended in 1856.

The old home of Ared Weeks is still there at 2090 Atlantic Avenue in the Town of Penfield but extensively remodeled since Underground times. Weeks was so rabid an abolitionist that he was expelled from the Baptist Church for his views. Penfield people believe he ran a station of the rail-less railroad.

The Negroes who found their way to Perinton and Penfield were bound for Rochester, the "Flour City," the milling center of America, and the boats that would bear them to Canada where there was no slavery.

Chapter 10

"Humanity's Friend"

On Harvey Blackmer's tombstone in the old Union Cemetery at Livonia are inscribed these words: "Humanity's Friend."

Harvey Blackmer was indeed a true friend of the Negro and a consistent foe of human slavery. His big farm on the northern edge of the village of Hemlock was a busy station on the Underground Railroad.

The handsome white house with its spacious grounds and many trees is still there, set well back from Route 15-A. It now is the home of Oscar Smith, prominent dairyman.

But the shacks that once stood in the woods on Blackmer land have been gone these 50 or more years. In those rude buildings many fearful Negro fugitives were hidden before they were transported to another station.

Frank Connor of Hemlock, Town of Livonia historian, recalls that old men told how when they were boys they sometimes rode on Blackmer's wagons that hauled hay to East Avon. Those loads of hay often concealed Negro slaves, on their way to Canada.

East Avon was at the junction of two principal roads. One led northward to Rochester whence many slaves escaped by boat to Canada. It also was on the east-west road across the state, the old Genesee Turnpike. Slaves could be taken eastward to Canandaigua whence the trail led through Wayne County to the Lake Ontario port of Pultneyville and westward to the Niagara, the short cut to Canada.

There is a tradition that the Taintor homestead at the northwest corner of the East Avon crossroads was an Underground depot. That handsome colonial-type landmark was recently torn down to make way for another gasoline station.

The Jacques farmhouse at the northwestern corner of Hemlock Lake, near its foot, according to Connor, was a haven for runaway slaves before it was enlarged and became a popular resort hotel. Russell R. Jacques built the farmhouse in 1851, when the Underground was just coming into flower.

There's a poignant story associated with the Jacques house. After her husband had been "sold down river," a distracted young Negro slave named Millie escaped with her infant son from a Southern plantation. While bloodhounds bayed in the distance, she and her babe hid in a swamp beside a narrow, swollen river, which divided free soil and slave territory.

Two men on the "free" side of the river saw the woman and sensed she was running away. One of them waded out into the river and directed her to toss the baby to him. The woman was told to cling to a tree limb overhanging the river, then swim across. She reached the other side safely.

The slave woman and her child landed in Underground hands and somehow found their way to Hemlock Lake and the Jacques place. She worked there until after the Civil

War. Then she went back South with her son in a vain effort to find her husband.

Thirty years later a Negro woman and a good-looking youth came to Hemlock on the stage and headed straight for the Jacques House on the lake. "Aunt Millie" and her son had made the long trip North so that her "baby" might meet the people who had befriended them in their hour of need. The son had become a prosperous cigar maker. Mother and son were warmly welcomed and spent a few days at the lakeside inn.

The only Livingston County Underground agent listed by W. H. Siebert in his *History of the Underground Railroad* is Col. Reuben Sleeper of Mount Morris. Although Sleeper is mentioned in old newspapers as president of the Livingston Anti-Slavery Society in the late 1850s, there is no record he ever ran an Underground depot.

Tradition links the National Hotel at Cuylerville with the Underground. The hotel was built in 1837 and was known as the National Exchange when an abolitionist, Truesdale Lamson, took it over in 1843. It is likely that he helped slaves on their way to freedom.

But the yarn that James G. Birney, the Presidential nominee of the Liberty Party in 1840 and 1844 and a converted slave owner, directed the movement of slaves from the hotel, does not hold up. It is true that Birney had Genesee Valley connections.

He married Elizabeth Fitzhugh, the sister of his college friend, Daniel Fitzhugh of Genesee and the daughter of Col. William Fitzhugh, who once owned slaves. It was at the Peterboro home of Elizabeth's sister, the wife of Gerrit Smith, the abolitionist leader, that the couple met. They were married in 1841 at the Groveland residence of Judge Charles Carroll in the presence of the Fitzhugh clan.

Birney, who died in 1857 after a long illness, is buried beside his Elizabeth in the Fitzhugh plot in the old cemetery at Williamsburg. But a study of his life shows that he never lived in the Valley, was only an occasional visitor there and a speaker at anti-slavery rallies all over the state.

He was too engrossed in national movements ever to be handling the movement of slaves on the Underground from a Cuylerville hotel.

Chapter 11

Of Hearses and Havens

William Marks Jr., "Uncle Billy" to all Naples, was a merchant who also ran an undertaking establishment. He had another sideline. It was operating a station of the Underground.

He was the only agent known to have transported fugitive slaves in a hearse. While his charges were in transit, he hid some of them in his coffins. The Negroes' fear of capture must have outweighed their inbred superstition. Otherwise they never could have been induced to get into such a compartment.

Marks took few villagers into his confidence. John P. Whiting, who made the coffins to order and the women of the Marks household who lined and trimmed them may have known the uses to which some of them were put. Other village women who worked on them did not.

"Uncle Billy" moved his runaways by night to Gideon Pitts's station at Honeoye and other places of refuge. No slave he harbored ever was recaptured although there are stories of narrow escapes.

Fantastic tales about the Marks station embellish the folklore of the countryside. One has to do with slave hunters who used bloodhounds. But somehow the dogs and their masters always arrived just after the Marks hearse had left for another station.

The story goes that none of the Negroes ever was hidden in the Marks house but all were admitted to the loft of his shop through a loosened plank in the roof. In the loft they slept on straw-covered planks. Embroidering the bloodhound story is the tradition that the straw on which they had slept was burned and the planks hidden. All this was to throw the dogs off the scent.

Some say one of the hearses he used on his Underground route is still stored in Naples. Other villagers tell you the Marks equipages were burned in a fire that ravaged his establishment years ago.

In 1834 Marks came from Connecticut to the Naples area as a young man. He began his business career as a pack peddler who for five years sold his wares from door to door, first on foot, later in a horse-drawn wagon. While peddling, he met his bride, Emily Holcomb, in a home near South Bristol where she was working as a seamstress.

After their marriage in 1839, he bought a share in a Naples store. Then he built his own place of business at Main and Mechanic Streets. He lived in a house in a rear of the store. That old dwelling, extensively remodeled and painted white, now is occupied by school teacher Theodore Harwood and his wife, Katherine, who maintains her dental office there.

A Negro couple who had been slaves, Edward and Addie Graham and their daughter, Rose, lived in the Marks home. Addie was a famous cook. Frederick Douglass once was a guest there.

Marks, a temperance zealot, once opened a tavern, "the New Temperance House," in competition with a village hotel that sold intoxicants.

In 1862, during the Civil War, when people were hoarding cash, he printed and issued over his signature his own paper money in small denominations. This scrip was accepted at his own store and at other establishments as cash.

"Uncle Billy" was a neat, smooth-shaven, medium-sized man, a devout Methodist. On his 60th birthday 300 townspeople turned out to honor him. He died in 1879 and sleeps in Rose Ridge Cemetery, his former vineyard which he gave the village as a burying ground and which got its name from the rose bushes he planted there.

Canandaigua was on the Underground route and tradition places several stations in the Ontario County shire town.

But their operators were exceptionally secretive because the only authenticated station was the old Dudley Tavern, also known as the Foster House, built in 1798 on the east side of South Main Street near the foot of Canandaigua Lake. It was removed from the scene long ago.

Nevertheless Canandaigua had its share of abolitionists. Probably the stations were not in the center of the town but, according to Underground procedure, on the outskirts.

Many slaves passed through Canandaigua, hidden in railroad baggage cars. They had been put on Northern Central trains at Elmira with the connivance of railroad employes. The cars were shifted at Canandaigua to the New York Central which was a direct link with the Niagara Frontier.

In the center of hill-surrounded Honeoye village stands a handsome home of colonial design. An historical marker tells the traveler that this is the Pitts Mansion, built in 1821 by Gideon Pitts Sr., son of Capt. Peter Pitts, the first settler in the place which first was known as Pitts Flats, then Pittstown, before it took the name of the inland lake the Indians called Honeoye.

The marker does not mention that this mansion also was the site of a noted Underground station operated by Gideon Pitts Jr. or that a daughter of his, Helen Pitts, became the second wife of Frederick Douglass, the Negro leader. It tells nothing of the sensation that marriage caused in Honeoye in 1884.

It is said that Helen Pitts was a child when Douglass came first to the homestead to confer with her father on Underground business.

All sorts of stories persist about Gideon Pitts's hiding places for fugitive slaves. According to one account, there was an unfinished cistern which never held any water but did shelter runaway Negroes. In the basement today is a walled-off room which might once have held a cistern.

There are five rooms in the cellar, along with a fireplace with Dutch oven before which fugitives may have warmed themselves in Underground days. There are bars on all the windows. There's a story that a tunnel led from the barn to that eerie basement.

The present owners are Mr. and Mrs. Leroy Sammis, who share the mansion with their daughter, Mrs. Kenneth Werder, and her husband.

According to a story handed down in the family of J. Sheldon Fisher, Ontario County historian, the homestead, built in 1811 by abolitionist Charles Fisher in Fishers, the village in the Town of Victor named for him, had an upper room accessible by a secret panel and used as a hideaway for runaway slaves.

Sheldon Fisher has on display on his rambling, three-story wooden Valenton Hall museum just off the Rochester-Victor Road a handcuff taken off a slave recaptured by abolitionists from officers who were taking him back South. The fugitive, who was a barber, gave his rescuers a straight razor as a token of his gratitude. These relics came to Historian Fisher from his grandfather.

A friend of the outcast and the oppressed and a fearless foe of slavery was a Phelps physician, Dr. Elias Willard Frisbie. He came to the village in 1819 to practice medicine with his father, Dr. William Frisbie. At first he settled in what was known as "the east village," where he kept extensive gardens.

Then he bought the Redfield property on the Clifton Springs Road west of Phelps and there he ran a busy Underground station. He also succored the homeless and alcoholics. He was an ardent champion of temperance and a candidate of the Liberty Party for Congress.

At a celebration of emancipation in the West Indies held in Geneva in 1840, Negroes of the area hired a band and staged a parade. In the procession marched but two white men, the Rev. Henry Bradley of Penn Yan and Dr. Frisbie. Both were subjected to ridicule from the white population.

The physician-humanitarian died in July, 1860, after being kicked by a horse he was treating in his door yard.

A volume, *When Phelps Was Young,* was published in 1939 when the community celebrated the sesquicentennial of its settlement. It contains the tale of a young Negro girl who had escaped from Alabama and was on her way to Canada to join a brother and who was sheltered for several days at an unidentified home in Phelps. Then she was taken to Rochester where she boarded a boat for Canada.

The town, into which years earlier the Southern settlers had brought their slaves, housed many abolitionists in the 1840s and 1850s.

Leman Hotchkiss Sr., Phelps miller and merchant lived on Eagle Street in a house with a fireplace in its basement, where, according to tradition, escaping slaves were warmed and fed. The original part of the old house was razed long ago. Leman was the father of two pioneers in the peppermint industry which once flourished in the Phelps-Lyons area.

There were two reputed stations at Nicholson's Corners, now Skuse's Corners, two miles north of Geneva on the Lyons Road. One was the stately brick house where the Nicholsons lived in Underground days and which now is the residence of Merlyn C. Phillips. The three basement fireplaces in the big house are said to have warmed fugitives traveling the freedom road.

Negroes also found asylum at the next farm to the southward where lived Gideon Palmer, son of a Quaker convert. A new house now stands on the site.

Friends of the Nicholsons and Palmers and fellow abolitionists were the Giffings of Geneva who lived on North Water Street (now Exchange) opposite the present St. Francis de Sales Church.

One night a gentle knock was heard at the Giffing door. There stood a Negro youth carrying a large and lumpy bag over his shoulder. Faint cries came from the bag.

In the house, the youth lowered the bag and untied its knots. The Giffings were startled when he lifted from it a tiny old woman. He said she was his mother, that they were bound for Canada and that she had become ill and too weak to walk any farther. So he put her into the bag and carried her for miles.

The family cared for the sick woman and hid her son. A young Giffing daughter carried food trays to them as she had for other refugees who came to the house. The child kept her lips sealed about the family's "visitors."

After some weeks mother and son left for Sodus Point.

They stopped at the Palmers and got a lift to the lakeside.

Before long the Giffings received a letter from the Negro youth telling of a safe arrival in Canada, of his mother's recovery and expressing deep gratitude for the kindness shown them in Geneva.

The Giffings had housed runaways before and would again but never did one arrive at their station in so strange a receptacle.

The family home is still standing but has been moved to the rear of a row of houses on Exchange Street.

When the old Van Houten house at 20 Pulteney St. in Geneva was being remodeled some years ago, a bullet hole was found in its front door. Back of it lies a story of Underground times.

The tale was told to Mrs. Frank H. Gilmore and her sister, Miss Josephine M. Johnson of 101 Washington St., by their grandmother Van Houten. Let Miss Johnson, a retired Batavia school teacher, tell the story:

"Grandma Van Houten was a little woman with a lot of spunk. She was a devout Methodist and believed in the Golden Rule.

"There were few homes then and many wooden fences and small gardens.

"Grandmother was sewing as usual by the window when she heard yelling and saw a Negro panting up the walk. She unlatched the door and fastened it again after letting him in.

"She grabbed part of a loaf of bread, let him out the back way and told him to clatter his heels on the fence so she would know he had gotten away.

"In the meantime shots were hitting the door and there was much to-do outside. Grandma unlatched the door, demanding to know why men were shooting at the house.

" 'You've got a nigger in there and you are hiding him,' one man said.

" 'Oh, no,' she replied. 'I would not have one in my house. I am a widow and all alone. But come in and search if you must.'

"She lighted a candle and encouraged the men to look into a loft over a lean-to. She admonished them: 'And don't you set fire to my house either.'

"Then she went back to her sewing. Finally the posse came downstairs. She threatened the law on them for 'invading the privacy of my home.'

"But she had heard the clatter of heels on the back fence!"

Chapter 12

The Trails of Wayne

Just east of Pultneyville, the picturesque village lapped by Ontario's waves, stands one of those blue state historical markers. On it is this legend:

"Site of Underground Railroad Terminus. Home of Samuel Cuyler used as terminus of Underground R.R. during slavery period."

The estate along the Lake Road, where the wealthy reformer sheltered many runaway slaves before they boarded ship for Canada now is a Wayne County park known as B. Forman Park, the gift of that late Rochester merchant, who bought it as a recreational place for his employes in the 1920s.

The house, which Cuyler bought in 1830 and to which he brought his bride two years later, burned years ago.

But the place lives in history as an important terminal of the invisible railroad. Pultneyville was a busy port in those days and some of the lake boats captains worked closely with Cuyler in getting fugitive slaves across Lake Ontario to Canada.

To the lakeside village ran the old post road from Canandaigua through Palmyra, Marion and Williamson. That road was dotted at intervals by Underground stations. There were others in the old Quaker settlements in Farmington, just over the line in Ontario County, and in the Town of Macedon, especially along the Victor Road.

Energetic, blue-eyed Samuel Cuyler, a powerful orator, was a strong advocate of temperance but abolition was the cause dearest to his heart.

As a state senator, in 1855, he introduced a bill which would give all residents the right to vote. Needless to say, it got few votes. Cuyler was variously a member of the Liberty, Free Soil and Republican parties.

He had many associates in the Underground movement. Among those listed in old Wayne County histories are William R. and Asa B. Smith of Macedon, Dr. Levi Gaylord and Dr. Cook of Sodus and Griffith Cooper, a noted Williamson Quaker.

Cuyler's eldest son, Ledyard, drove many wagon loads of slaves from Sodus and other points to his father's estate—never by daylight.

A staunch ally was Capt. Horatio N. Throop, one of the leading Pultneyville lake captains. For years he ran sail and steam boats on the lake. He helped design and commanded the steamer, *Ontario,* pride of the lake fleet.

The story goes that Cuyler would take his fugitives to Throop and say: "I have some passengers for you." The captain's invariable reply was: "My boat runs for passengers." Unquestionably he helped many Negroes to escape to Canada.

Associated with him in his shipping business and other enterprises was his brother, Washington S. Throop, although it is not certain that he helped fugitive slaves escape.

Throop's nephew, James T. Holling, also a lake boat captain, once dropped off slaves on Presque Isle in the lake opposite Pultneyville. When the Negroes realized they were on Canadian soil, they knelt in grateful prayer.

There's a tradition that runaways were taken to the piers opposite the Jeremiah Selby house, built in 1808 and still standing at Jay and Washington Streets, where they were hidden among piles of wood.

A reputed hiding place for slaves is an old wooden wing in the rear of the brick house on Washington Street now occupied by the Alan Hasselwanders.

A well-known station on the Marion Post Road south of the village of Williamson and only five miles from the lake was maintained by the mild-mannered Quaker, Griffith Cooper, who at heart was a flaming liberal. The farm house, built of field stone with walls 18 inches thick, is still there, on an eminence set well back from the highway. Its outer walls were covered with plaster some years ago.

Until this summer Mr. and Mrs. Ernest Oakleaf lived there. Mrs. Oakleaf's grandfather, Brutus Wilder, bought it from Griffith Cooper. It then passed into the hands of Wilder's son-in-law, Sidney D. Milhan. Mrs. Oakleaf's grandmother lived in the stone house for more than 80 years. It is known in the neighborhood as the Milhan place.

In the old house is a secret chamber where Cooper hid fugitive slaves. When David Oakleaf, a son of Mr. and Mrs. Ernest Oakleaf, then a high school student, wrote in 1956 a prize essay on local operations of the Underground, a highlight of his paper dealt with his investigation of the hiding place in the attic of the family home.

First he discovered small doors on the east and west sides, each blocked by a big box. These doors led to a triangular hall-like space where the roof sloped down. Crawling along the passageways, David came to a recess

77

or cranny where eight or ten persons could be jammed in.

That was Griffith Cooper's slave hide-away and he made sure it was a safe one.

David Oakleaf wrote that his grandmother told him a tale of slave hunters coming to the farm, seeking runaway Negroes. They drove swords into a load of hay in which they believed slaves were concealed. They left empty-handed. But there had been several Negroes in that load of hay and one of them was stabbed severely—but he made no outcry.

Griffith Cooper was a true friend of the Indians, as well as of the Negroes. When a land company tried to engineer a gigantic steal of Indian lands, Cooper carried the fight right to the White House and to the President, who was his friend. When Martin Van Buren told Cooper: "Griffith, the white men need these lands," the Williamson Quaker replied quietly: "Martin, thee knows that it is not so."

Nevertheless the Indians lost a large chunk of their reservation land.

Dr. Gaylord of Sodus who aided Cuyler's Underground operations was read out of his church for his abolitionist views but was reinstated. Garrett Smith of Sodus also was reputedly associated with the movement.

A story has been handed down that slaves were hidden in the woods on the bluff which now is part of the Sodus Fruit Farm on the Lake Road. Ships out of Sodus Point carried slaves across the lake but that port was not as important in the Underground setup as Pultneyville.

Two houses on the Macedon-Victor Road in the old Macedon Quaker settlement have been pointed out as Underground stations. One, known as the Reeve place, built in 1810, had a kitchen basement with a double fire-place and several curious small rooms. The rear part of the once 12-room house had been torn down. Once there was a large hole 20 feet southeast of the house which has been filled in with stones. This may have been another hideout for fugitives.

North of the Reeve place on the opposite side of the road, set back among a cluster of fir trees, is a white colonial type house, another reputed station. It was once the home of the Rev. Arnold Bristol, a Quaker preacher. It is said that years ago the cellar housed a series of stalls which were hiding places for slaves.

Among residents of the Macedon area who were abolitionists were Jacob Smith, a miller-blacksmith who lived on what is now called the Blue Bell Island farm on the Marion-Macedon Road; Durfee Herendeen, who was a large wheat grower but because of his temperance beliefs, never raised barley; and Ira Lapham. Whether these men harbored fugitive slaves is purely a matter of conjecture.

At 322 Main Street in the historic village of Palmyra an historical marker stands in front of a sturdy 126-year-old gray brick house with brown trim. It designates the old home of the Quaker jeweler, Pliny Sexton Sr., as an Underground Railroad station. It is said Sexton hid Negroes in loads of hay and produce and took them to the next station on the route that led to the lake.

Stationmaster Sexton's son, Pliny T., was an eminent lawyer and banker who was once chancellor of the State Board of Regents and who gave Palmyra its village park.

In the shire town of Lyons, on the west side of William Street, the home of Columbus Croul, a blacksmith who shod horses that hauled the Erie Canal boats, was an Underground station. Its basement had many small compartments with shower baths supplied by a water tank on the main floor. If the story is true, this station provided "luxury" accommodations accorded few Negroes who followed the North Star.

In May, 1860, the *Lyons Democrat Press* informed its readers that "there is in our pleasant village a place where a fugitive slave was kept from Saturday to Tuesday and citizens raised funds for him." No names were mentioned.

Chapter 13

22 Days in a Box

In 1851 two brothers moved from Connecticut to Washington, D.C., where they became market gardeners. For helpers they hired a few slaves from their masters by the day.

They had not been in the business long before one of their hands, a young Negro woman, came to them in tears. Her story was a sad one. Her husband and a son had been sold "down the river," leaving her with a seven-year-old daughter who helped in the Yankees' gardens and was a great favorite with them. Now, the mother said, she had learned through the "grapevine" of her people that she was about to be sold down South and separated from her remaining child.

The Connecticut brothers, abolitionists at heart, devised an escape plan. They made a large wooden box which would fit into the broad wagon in which they hauled their vegetables to the city markets. Into the box they put some straw, food, a jug of water. The mother and child climbed into the box and the cover was nailed down. Apertures had been made in the sides of the box for ventilation.

So, with one brother driving the team, a long, strange journey began at night. The other brother stayed in Washington, so no suspicion would be aroused by the absence of both at the same time.

The next morning found the wagon 40 miles into Maryland. The driver looked after the needs of his charges in isolated places at night. When they passed through towns, the mother hushed the prattle of the little girl.

Across Maryland and into Pennsylvania, over the mountain roads into Western New York, the wagon rumbled on. On the twenty-second day of its journey, it reached its destination, the home of Isaac Phelps on Warsaw's West Hill. Phelps, who knew the Connecticut brothers, had housed runaway slaves before and he would again.

The box was opened and the woman and child released from their cramped quarters. Both were tired and their bones ached from lying in the same position so many hours. But they were in good spirits and soon recovered. The next day their deliverer began the long journey back to Washington.

The fugitives were secreted for three weeks, part of the time in Arcade, until it was felt all fear of pursuit had passed. Then they returned to Warsaw where the mother obtained work. In four months she gave birth to another daughter. Within a year she died of tuberculosis.

The older girl was brought up in the home of Allen Breck, a Warsaw business man. She became the wife of William Burghardt, a respected Negro resident. The baby was adopted by another family.

The slave owner in Washington never found out what had become of his human chattels.

Other Wyoming County men besides Isaac Phelps harbored runaway slaves in defiance of the law. A chain of Underground stations wound through Warsaw, Sheldon, Arcade, Perry, Attica, Pearl Creek, Wyoming and other places. The routes were flexible and the identity of few of the station masters has been established.

But without question many a fugitive Negro, following the North Star, traveled the invisible railway to the home of Michael Smallwood on Warsaw's East Hill.

Smallwood came to the United States in 1819 from his native Yorkshire in England and lived briefly in Virginia, where he developed an abiding repugnance for human slavery. After a short residence in York, Livingston County, he settled in 1823 on towering East Hill, where he built a log cabin in the woods. That was replaced by the homestead along Smallwood Road, which burned several years ago.

He hid slaves in a nearby swamp, as well as in the cellar of his home. There is a tale handed down in the family that when the slave hunters came to East Hill, Smallwood's wife, Elizabeth, would rock serenely in a chair placed on a rug squarely over the trap door which led to the cellar where slaves were secreted.

Michael Smallwood, who founded a notable family line, died in 1867. He flaunted his abolitionist activities and it was his wish that on his tombstone these words be inscribed: "He was a friend of the slave."

Warsaw also was for many years the home of a national leader in the anti-slavery movement. He was Seth Merrill Gates, who while a resident of Le Roy, served two spectacular terms in Congress, from 1838 to 1842 as an Anti-Slavery Whig.

At the request of his friend, John Quincy Adams, he drew up a protest, which was signed by all anti-slavery Congressmen, branding the annexation of Texas as a covert move to extend slavery. That action has been called the first organized effort in Congress to check the spread of slavery and it won for Gates the hatred of many Southern politicians. A Savannah planter offered a reward of $500 for the delivery of Seth Gates, dead or alive, in that Georgia city.

In 1844 at the close of his Congressional career, Gates bought the stately house at 15 Perry Ave. in Warsaw, which is the present headquarters of the Warsaw Historical Society. There he lived until his death in 1887. The many-windowed mansion with its Colonial lines is a museum for historical objects, as well as a meeting place.

In Warsaw Gates abandoned the practice of law to go into business. He was the Free Soil party candidate for lieutenant governor in 1848 and ran well ahead of his ticket. He later joined the Republican Party and was nominated by Lincoln as Warsaw postmaster.

Early in his career he had been a leader in the Anti-Masonic movement and was identified with the temperance cause all his life.

But it was as a flaming champion of abolition that Seth Gates won national renown. While he was deeply involved in the Underground movement, it is doubtful that, despite local tradition, he ever dared to hide fugitives in his own home. That would be the first place in Warsaw slave hunters would head for.

It is more likely that the residence of his brother, Chauncey, which still stands on East Genesee Street, the present home of Grant Hume, was an Underground hideaway.

For generations Humphreys have been leaders in Wyoming County business and public affairs. One of the clan, Lester Humphrey, a native of Connecticut, settled in 1819 in what was known as Humphrey Hollow, east of Sheldon Center in the Town of Sheldon. There he ran a farm and a saw mill—and a station of the Underground. It is probable that the slaves were sent from Sheldon to Arcade and thence to Warsaw or Attica on their way to the international border.

In his *History of the Underground Railroad,* Wilbur H. Siebert lists these Warsaw men as station operators: Dr. Augustus Frank, physician-business man; F. C. D. McKay and Andrew W. Young, a local historian-author. While these men were identified with the anti-slavery cause there is no tangible evidence any of them housed fugitive slaves. If they did, it was a well-kept secret.

Warsaw may well claim to be the birthplace of the Liberty Party, the rallying point for the opponents of the extension of slavery. On Nov. 13, 1839, two years before Wyoming County was carved from old Genesee, the Western New York Anti-Slavery Society, meeting in the Warsaw Presbyterian Church, nominated James G. Birney for President. The Rochester reformer, Myron Holley, dominated that meeting.

No new party was organized at the time and Birney, a noted abolitionist who once had owned slaves, believed the third party movement "premature." He declined the Warsaw nomination but in April, 1840, in Albany he was formally nominated as the Presidential candidate of the new Liberty Party.

He received less than 7,000 votes in the national election that Fall. In 1844 when he was again the Liberty Party candidate, it was a different story. Birney rolled up a national total of 62,000 votes. The 15,000 ballots cast for him in New York swung that pivotal state into the Polk column and probably cost the Whig candidate, Henry Clay, the Presidency.

So in Warsaw in 1839 had been sown the seeds of a powerful new third party, the forerunner of the Republican Party.

Arcade, originally China, was another anti-slavery hot-bed and a key link in the Underground chain. The Arcade abolition leaders were Col. Charles O. Shepard and Ralston W. Lyman, an in-law.

On Jan. 28, 1840 what amounted to a state anti-slavery convention was held in the old Congregational Church in Arcade and plans laid for the Albany meeting at which the Liberty Party was founded. Col. Shepard presided at the session in Arcade. He later became a founder of the Republican Party in the state.

Enemies of the abolitionist cause jeeringly called Arcade "Niggerville" because of its Underground and anti-slavery connections. One route of the invisible railway led into Arcade from Franklinville in Cattaraugus County and the other over the hills from Rushford in Allegany County. The latter must have passed through my birthplace, Sandusky, although I never heard of any Underground activities in that small village.

There were several "known" stations in Arcade. Probably the West Main Street home of Col. Charles Shepard was not one of them. He was far too prominent in the movement. But it is said that his life was threatened more than once by hot-headed Southerners who came to "Niggerville" in quest of their human chattels. Among guests at the Shepard home were Frederick Douglass and the talented Negro clergyman, the Rev. Samuel R. Ward.

Undoubtedly the R. W. Lyman house on Church Street on the banks of the Cattaraugus Creek was a haven for fugitive slaves, as was the woolen mill of Horatio N. Waldo, a known "conductor" of the UGRR.

Another reputed hiding place was the windowless attic of the Samuel Tilden home on North Street. A house at Main and Water Streets and another opposite the old

Arcade High School on West Main Street also were said to have been stations, although no data is available on their occupants in Underground days.

Harry S. Douglass, Wyoming County historian, wrote that the late Miss Catherine Eastman of Attica, once told him that her grandfather, Matthew Eastman, hid many an escaped slave on his farm, three and one half miles south of the village of Attica. Presumably those Negroes came from the Sheldon station.

The late George S. Brooks of Groton, magazine writer and playwright, was proud of the part his pioneer forebears at Pearl Creek, his birthplace, played in the Underground drama. A letter from him on file in the Historical Center at Geneseo told that his grandfather, Hugh T. Brooks, maintained a haven for slaves at the family homestead in the Town of Covington from 1851 to 1861, with the exception of three years.

In that interim, because of the objections of Benedict Brooks, Hugh's father, the station was housed in the Hall cottage in Wyoming Village. The old man, who feared anti-slavery agitation would bring war, later relented and operations were resumed at Pearl Creek.

George Brooks wrote that the Negroes were brought to Pearl Creek from Portageville and that some of them were taken to Lima, on the main road to Canandaigua, whence they used the Palmyra-Williamson route to Lake Ontario. But other sources maintain that the next station after Pearl Creek was the one on the outskirts of nearby Le Roy.

Siebert listed as an Underground conductor Josiah Andrews of Perry, the village orator and poet. When the Genesee County Anti-Slavery Society was organized at Warsaw in 1836, it was voted to establish an abolitionist paper, the *American Citizen,* at Warsaw. After it was published for one year in Warsaw, Andrews moved it to Perry and kept it going until 1841 when it was re-established in Rochester.

Andrews, who was also a temperance zealot, bought the National Hotel in Perry solely to convert it into a temperance house.

Chapter 14

"The Medicine Man"

Around 1856 a six-foot Scot with piercing black eyes and boundless energy appeared in the Le Roy area. His name was Daniel MacDonald and he was an ordained minister. But he did no preaching in the neighborhood.

Instead, on the Keeney Road, two and one half miles north-west of Le Roy, he set up a shop where he made proprietary medicines by day. His nocturnal activities are more pertinent to this story.

On a neighboring farm lived Elijah Huftelen, a teenager, who got to know the tall Scot. The youth sensed an aura of mystery about the newcomer, who was pleasant mannered but never talked about himself.

Elijah wondered why MacDonald at all times kept at least three horses in his barn, although he never used all of them—in the daytime, at least. And never did the preacher–medicine man ever own a gray or white horse.

The farm boy's wonderment grew when one day Mac-Donald, saying he was likely to be called away at any hour of the night, asked Elijah to take care of any of his horses left behind. Sometimes he was gone for days.

One day the youth saw MacDonald in earnest conversation under an apple tree with four Negroes, two women, a man and a boy of about 13. The Scot borrowed a big wagon and when darkness fell he loaded the four blacks into it and drove away. He did not return for two days.

Before MacDonald left, he confided to Elijah the secret of his mysterious trips. Daniel MacDonald was the operator of the Le Roy station of the Underground Railroad and his medicine shop was only a blind. In later days Huftelen saw more than one furtive Negro come up the road, asking "where medicine man live?"

MacDonald wanted no light-colored horses in his stables because they would be too conspicuous at night.

Young Huftelen won the older man's complete confidence and became his assistant on the Underground. For five years the pair helped many a runaway slave along the freedom road.

About the turn of this century, Elijah Huftelen, by then an aging orchardist living in a stone house on the Butler Road, north of Le Roy, published locally two small books which told in dramatic detail many of his experiences as an agent of the Underground. Copies of his *The Underground Railroad* and *Lights on the Underground* are collectors' items today.

Huftelen wrote that the Le Roy station was on "the Covington Route," which presumably led through Arcade, Sheldon and Warsaw before entering Genesee County from the Town of Covington. Then it led to Pavilion Center, followed the south side of the Oatka Creek, skirting Le Roy village. From the MacDonald station the fugitives were taken to Morganville, past Horseshoe Lake, to the five corners on the line between Elba and Batavia Townships, whence the trail led to the Niagara.

According to Huftelen, the slaves traveled in small groups, often singly and in pairs. Usually they came at night to the door of "the medicine man."

MacDonald sometimes used a "rockaway" carriage with oil-cloth curtains which could be let down from the top and buttoned to the sides of the carriage box, effectively hiding the occupants. Often the operators drove all night, changing horses at stations along the way.

One visitor was etched indelibly on Huftelen's memory. One night in 1858 an aging vender of medicines and extracts, a genial but earnest white man named Thaddeus Fitch, stayed at the MacDonald station. He said his real mission was carrying messages to relatives in the South from fugitives who had reached Canada.

He told the boy in somber tones: "This will be my last trip. I see within five years the shadow of great armies and the Underground will be only a memory." Thaddeus Fitch did not live to see his prophecy come true. He died in 1859.

One night three Negroes, one a dark-skinned woman with a 12-year-old son and the third, to all appearances, a slim, roughly dressed youth, arrived at the station. The woman, vowing she would join her husband in Canada, showed Huftelen a wicked-looking bowie knife concealed in her clothes.

The next midnight the three were put in a light covered wagon, bound for the Pembroke station. Reaching out by lantern light to shake hands with the "young man," Huftelen chanced to glance up the fugitive's sleeve and saw a shapely arm, as white as his own. He told MacDonald this runaway was a woman in disguise. The medicine man asked some questions, then drove away with the three slaves, who eventually made their way across the international border.

Back of "the young man with the shapely white arm," lay a strange story. The fugitive was a mulatto slave girl, handsome, intelligent and so light-skinned she passed as white. A rich planter became enamored of her and tried to buy her from her owners, who had treated her kindly, but refused to sell her.

The infatuated planter connived at her escape via the invisible railroad. He arranged that she visit the cabin of a free Negress, whence she emerged, dressed in man's clothes, her long hair cut short, her skin stained dark. She was taken to a meeting place with the Negress with the young boy, and the three found their way to Le Roy.

The planter found employment for the girl with a family in Montreal. Her lover spent every Summer with her and two children were born to them. When he died in 1879, he bequeathed the children $2,500 each and their mother $5,000.

In 1888 business took Huftelen to Montreal. He looked up the woman whose strange story was well known in the Canadian city. He found a white-haired, distinguished-looking woman with charming manners. After 32 years she recognized him "because of your sharp eyes which looked up my sleeve that night in Le Roy."

A minor mishap necessitated a change in the Genesee County route around 1859. One night, when MacDonald was taking two Negro men westward on the Batavia-Elba road in a carriage, a linch pin slipped out and a wheel came off the vehicle.

While the occupants were searching the road for the vital pin, a coon dog came charging out from a field and made for the Negroes. One of the terrified men caught the dog by its hind legs and banged the animal down on the road with such force that every bone in the beast's body was broken. Then he tossed the dead dog over a fence.

Within a few minutes a party of hunters came along and asked if anyone had seen a dog. They were told a dog had been seen running down the road. Just then the missing pin was found, put back in place and the carriage rolled on. The incident worried MacDonald.

His worry was justified. Two days later the dog's body was found. The hunters, who had been suspicious all the time of the presence of a carriage on a dark road and of its Negro occupants, although they did not know MacDonald, connected the killing of the dog to the UGRR and reported the incident to the officers of the law.

The route was hastily changed. The Le Roy station was shifted to Bowmansville and on a new route which led from Friendship in Allegany County, to Holland, Elma and Lancaster to Bowmansville. Huftelen remained with MacDonald at the new haven.

Despite the change in the route reported by Huftelen, there is evidence that Underground operations continued in the Wyoming area, at least, until the Civil War began.

Another mishap caused a swift change in plans of Underground operatives in Pittsburgh after the body of a white spy who had stained his skin black was found floating in a river. It was believed he knew about 13 runaway slaves then concealed in Pittsburgh.

So the UGRR shipped them out, in twos and threes, every third night, to Olean. From there two were sent to Rochester, two to Lewiston, two to Black Rock (Buffalo) and the other seven over "the long route" to Ithaca, thence north to the St. Lawrence, after a stopover at Gerrit Smith's Peterboro sanctuary.

Huftelen also chronicled another unusual escape in which a Rochester woman played a prominent role. In the Summer of 1860 there arrived at the Bowmansville station a Negress, her 11-year-old daughter and teen-age stepson, a handsome boy so light of skin he could pass as white.

The owner of this trio, a wealthy, young Virginia widow, valued them highly, especially the handsome boy. She spread the alarm and the slave catchers were hot on the runaway's trail.

MacDonald managed to get the mother and daughter across the Niagara at Lewiston by some fast driving, but did not dare to try to pass the boy at that point. Instead he was taken to Rochester in a carriage.

Douglass, the Rochester stationmaster, was in Washington, but a Mrs. Fair took charge, dressed the youth in girl's clothes, raised money for his fare, stained him black, and took him, disguised as her maid, on a Toronto-bound boat. The officers and slave catchers were fooled by the disguise and the next day he joined his mother and sister at Lewiston.

Often a turn in the Underground route was indicated by a branch, two feet tall, stuck in the ground close to the road. One night in 1858, three fugitives missed the marker which pointed the way to the MacDonald station and landed in the village of Le Roy.

A free Negro who lived in Le Roy took them to his employer, J. R. Anderson, who lived at the top of the Lake Street hill. Anderson, a brusque and vigorous man, was no friend of slavery, although not connected with the UGRR.

After feeding the three Negroes, he pushed them into his sleigh, shouting, "pile in, boys, all hell can't get you now!" and drove them to Bergen. Thence they were taken to Rochester where Douglass got them across the border.

Le Roy was an early center of the anti-slavery movement, abolitionist meetings were held there often and fugitive slaves were hidden in the area long before MacDonald set up his station.

In 1878 the *Le Roy Gazette* published an interview with

Samuel Grannis, an erstwhile hardware merchant in Le Roy. He had moved to Hammondsport and during a visit to his former home town, the old man revealed that in 1833 he had run an Underground station in a stone building on "The Dock" beside the Oatka, the present village postoffice site.

George Tomlinson of Perry, a former Le Royan, in his reminiscences published after the Civil War, named Grannis as one of four active abolitionists in the Le Roy of the 1830s. The others were Judge Henry Brewster, Deacon Samuel Comstock and Congressman Seth M. Gates, whose remarkable career is discussed elsewhere.

Tomlinson also wrote of an early slave hunt in the area. A Le Roy–bound fugitive got off the trail and landed in Avon. His owner was hot on his trail and after hearing reports that the Negro had been seen trudging along the Avon–Le Roy road, recruited some men with fast horses to track the man down. The hunt was futile. The Negro had been "swallowed up" somewhere along the line, and the slaver had to return South, empty handed. It came out later that the Negro had been hidden for 10 days by an abolitionist whose identity was never revealed.

Richard Selden, supervisor of the Town of Le Roy, tells an unusual story of the Underground time, involving his grandfather, Richard Lord Selden, also a one time Le Roy supervisor. One day in the late 1850s the elder Selden was working around his barn when a disheveled and obviously frightened Negro approached him and asked, "which way north?"

Selden, who was not connected with the Underground but was a friend of the underdog, pointed toward a swamp near the Griswold Road and watched the Negro disappear in that direction.

In a few minutes, two U.S. marshals drove up to the Selden home, saying they were looking for a fugitive slave and asked if a Negro had been seen in the neighborhood. Selden told them he had seen a black man heading north.

The marshals ordered Selden to get into their buggy. They drove down a dead-end lane. When they had to stop, they spotted the Negro running across the fields toward the swamp. All three began chasing him on foot. Selden outran his older, stouter, companions and caught up with the hunted man, over a ridge and out of sight of the federal men. He told the Negro to follow a brook into the swamp until he reached a large pool and to wait for him there until darkness came.

Returning to the winded marshals, Selden told them the Negro had disappeared in a thick swamp and that if they drove to a certain opening, they could easily nab him when he came out. He put them miles off the trail. That was the last he saw of the marshals.

After dark Selden took food, shoes and clothing to the Negro cowering beside the pool and then drove him to Elba, whence the UGRR saw that he reached Canada safely.

But that's not the end of the story.

Around 1880, Richard Lord Selden, who had fought for the Union and held several town offices, made a business trip to Baltimore. He put up at a good hotel. He noticed that the personable Negro who waited on him at dinner gave him special attention.

After two more meals, during which the waiter anticipated Selden's every want, the Negro asked the Le Roy man if he remembered him. Selden could not recall ever seeing him before. Then the Negro identified himself as the fugitive Selden had rescued nearly 30 years earlier.

The waiter had returned to the States from Canada and during the war had enlisted in a Negro regiment, the one, which after surrendering to General Forrest at Fort Pillow, was mercilessly slaughtered by Confederates, infuriated at the sight of Negroes in Union blue. The waiter had been one of only 14 in the whole regiment who was spared.

Chapter 15

On to the Niagara

Just across the Niagara River lay Canada, "the Promised Land of Freedom" of which bent, wizened Harriet Tubman sang as she led her bands of footsore, frightened fugitives out of bondage.

So the Niagara Frontier became the Mecca of thousands of Negroes who "rode" the Underground Railroad. Buffalo, Black Rock, Niagara Falls and Lewiston were the principal escape hatches.

But because the slave hunters watched those key ports closely many of the Underground stations were in nearby interior towns.

The UGRR routes which converged on the Niagara led through Chautauqua, Cattaraugus, Allegany, Genesee, Orleans, Niagara and other Western New York counties, as well as Erie County south of the key ports.

The Niagara River ferry at Black Rock, now a part of the city of Buffalo, was a widely-used means of egress. Where the river was narrow, rowboats took many slaves across to Canada, the land where all humans were free.

Ingenious devices were used to get runaways across to the free soil of Canada. Some operator rigged up a contraption, consisting of a crockery crate with a false bottom where slaves could be secreted and which could be hauled or pushed across the frozen river.

Wagons carrying grist to mills along the river also had false bottoms and under the grain many a slave was safely hidden.

It is not recorded that any escapes were made in the fashion of Eliza in the book, *Uncle Tom's Cabin*, by leaping from one block of drifting ice to the next one.

Interior Erie County was dotted with stations. One was as far south as Rice Corners in the Town of Sardinia. It was run by farmer John Wilkes. His daughter, Mary Wilkes Furias, used to tell stories of the Underground to her grandniece, Mrs. Elwood G. Wagner of Arcade.

When Mrs. Furias was a child, she heard on many a night a low rap at the door of their home. Her father would go outside and immediately return, put on warm clothing and gather up some blankets.

Then he would leave without telling his destination or the reason for his sudden departure. In the morning his team would be weary and his vehicles spattered with dirt or snow.

In later years her father told Mrs. Furias that he took slaves to the next Underground station, at Holland, where the operator was Abner Orr. Thence they were sent on to another depot at South Wales after a night's rest.

Springville reputedly housed at least two Underground stations. About one house at Middle Road and Vaughan Street, now occupied by Mildred Vaughan, lingers an odd tale. Escaping slaves were concealed in an upstairs room where the high headboard of a bed formed a barrier to the only door in the chamber. Other stations were said to have been operated at Sharp and Buffalo Roads and at the Frye farm in nearby Zoar.

Harold E. Clark of Buffalo recalls that his grandfather, Roswell Hill, who died in 1890, told him that his old home at Eden was one of the last stations south of the Niagara.

The house, still in the family, has been extensively remodeled since Underground days.

There is little doubt that the homestead at East Quaker Street and Baker Road in Orchard Park which Quaker abolitionist Obadiah Baker built in 1840 was a station. Baker, an early settler, donated the land for the Quaker meeting house and cemetery. Wherever there was a Quaker settlement, there also were plenty of abolitionist workers.

In historic Town Line, the village which splits the Towns of Lancaster and Alden, the barn loft of Mary Willis, an Alfred College alumna who married a Webster, was a supposed hiding place for fugitive Negroes.

Oddly enough, Town Line is the community which in 1861 voted to "secede" from the Union and which held many Rebel sympathizers. It was "readmitted" in 1945 as a combination newspaper and movie publicity stunt, which attracted wide attention.

The trail to the Niagara also led through Orleans and Niagara Counties. According to a story handed down in the family, Robert Anderson hid runaway slaves in the cobblestone house one mile west of Gaines in Orleans County now occupied by Earl Priestly. The place contains a large basement fireplace.

Underground lore also clings to the brick and frame house in Barre Center, four miles south of Albion. It once was a tavern. A former owner, Carl Hakes, some years ago on opening what was believed to be a cupboard door, found steep stairs leading to the attic.

At the top of these stairs was a brick walled cell-like compartment under the ridge pole. It could have been an Underground hideout, although some local historians incline to the theory it was a meeting place for a Masonic lodge when that order "went underground" after the furor caused by the disappearance of William Morgan, who exposed the secrets of the fraternity.

In Niagara County among the early settlers of Lockport, Somerset, Hartland and Royalton were many Quakers who were staunch friends of the Negro.

In 1830, long before the Underground was in full swing, two professional slave catchers came to Lockport in search of a runaway slave. They could not find him but seized a popular barber and tried to take him back South. He was rescued by workmen on the Erie Canal, led by Quaker Darius Comstock. Comstock asserted that "this man will never be taken from Lockport" and demanded a legal hearing. A justice of the peace ordered the barber discharged and the slave catchers left without any victim.

But abolitionism met popular disfavor in Lockport, as it did in many other communities. In July, 1834, when the abolitionists held a meeting in the Court House, the speaker was heckled so vigorously that he could not be heard and the gathering broke up in disorder. In 1836 a crowd broke up another abolitionist rally in the Presbyterian Church.

Some 40 Presbyterians withdrew from that denomination and formed a Congregational society. The slavery issue also divided the Lockport Universalists. Abolitionism disrupted many churches in the early time.

When the Underground began to operate on a large scale in the 1850s, Lockport became a haven for many runaways although only one station can be authenticated.

That was the now vacant stone house beside the Erie Canal at the end of Summit Street. During the heyday of the UGRR it was the home of Francis Hichens, who had been a canal contractor and who ran a glass factory. This house contained a secret stairway leading to a third floor hiding place.

Hichens in 1861 was instrumental in saving from bondage a free Lockport Negro who had worked for him. This Negro with the resounding name of Chancellor Livingstone had been enticed to Kentucky to work on a farm in the belief that the border state was free soil. Anyhow he was a free Negro so he thought he had nothing to fear.

Despite "the free papers" he carried, his Southern employer declared Chancellor was his slave. Hichens set legal machinery in motion to prove that the man was a free Negro and succeeded in getting him safely back to Lockport. Hichens also obtained the arrest of the slaver who had lured the Negro to Kentucky on false pretenses.

In the 1850s an undetermined number of slaves bound for Canada passed through Lockport on Erie Canal boats. Most of them got on at Albany, terminus of an Eastern Underground route. Canal boat owners and captains friendly to the cause co-operated in carrying the slaves. Some of the escapees stopped off in Lockport, whence they made their way across the Niagara to Canada.

Two influential leaders among the abolitionists were Lyman H. Spalding, a merchant, and Moses Richardson, editor of the *Lockport Daily Journal*. It has not been established that either sheltered slaves on their property but they gave financial aid and prestige to the movement.

Newark, now Niagara-on-the-Lake, in the province of Ontario, was a popular rendezvous for runaway Negroes. While there was a bridge across the Niagara at Lewiston, connecting the two nations in the 1850's, few slaves dared to cross it because it was so closely watched. Instead most of them were rowed across the river at its narrow points.

Lockport demonstrated its generous spirit in the case of

a smart and personable young Negro known as "Gentleman George" Groins. One of a family of nine, he had escaped from North Carolina with a price of $1,000 on his head. He got away through an ingenious ruse. While running errands for his master, he had access to the Court House. He got hold of "free papers," and the required seal and used them to get across the Mason-Dixon line.

He reached Wisconsin where abolitionists bought his freedom for $500. Around 1852 he landed in Lockport and became an omnibus driver for the Tremont House, on the site of the present Lox Plaza. He was a persuasive talker, obtained many passengers and saved his money.

When the Tremont burned in the big fire of 1854, "Gentleman George" lost his $300 savings in the blaze. He had been putting the money aside to buy the freedom of his mother and a 14-year-old brother in North Carolina. His goal was $900.

His friends in Lockport put on a benefit performance and raised $1,070. A leader in the campaign, Judge Jonathan L. Wood, went to Carolina and managed the release of George's mother and brother.

The most famous Underground station on the Niagara was the massive stone house on the river bank about one half mile north of Lewiston and known as "Tryon's Folly."

It was built by Amos Tryon who settled in Lewiston about 1815. He became a prosperous merchant and married the sister of Benjamin Barton, one of the proprietors of the enormously profitable Niagara portage.

Tryon decided to build a grand new house on the river. But his wife preferred to reside in the village despite the noble dimensions of the new house on the Niagara and its superb view. The strong-minded Mrs. Tryon refused to move and the couple stayed in Lewiston.

Spiders spun their webs in the unoccupied stone mansion which was set back from the road and hidden by shrubbery until Josiah Tryon, brother of Amos and pastor of the Lewiston Presbyterian Church, found a use for it. The Rev. Mr. Tryon was the local agent for the Underground and "Tryon's Folly" got some new inhabitants. None of them stayed very long. They were fugitive slaves.

The place was ideally located as a hideout and a getaway point. It stood on the high bank of the river, had four levels below the main floor and was built on a terrace-type design with graduated extensions under the river side of the mansion.

From the upper basement a passageway reached the third level from which one descended by a ladder to the last level and thence to the bank of the river a few feet above the water.

Josiah Tryon, who had the assistance of other ministers and abolitionists in the community, got many Negroes across the river by boat. When word got around that there were slave hunters in the neighborhood, the escapees were hidden in the various basements of the stone house until the coast was clear and they could be rowed across the Niagara by night.

In post-Underground days, flickering lights seen in the mansion gave rise to the belief it was used by smugglers. The long vacant building became known as a "haunted house."

In 1912 one wing of the building was burned. Around 1915 it was purchased by John L. Harper of Niagara Falls who rebuilt the fire-wrecked section. Since then there have been several occupants. Now "Tryon's Folly," no longer a hideaway for slaves, a haven for smugglers or a "haunted house," is the pleasant riverside home of Dr. John W. Owen, a Niagara Falls dentist.

*　　*　　*

Although relatively few Underground stations have been authenticated in Buffalo proper, the lakeport is invested with a mass of lore connected with the invisible railway and abolition.

As early as 1838 two sleigh loads of Negro fugitives were brought from Ohio's Western Reserve to his father's new home in Buffalo, Prof. Edward Orton was to recall in later years. The slaves were bound for Canada.

There is no question about the important role played in the Underground drama by the red brick Michigan Avenue Baptist Church. In 1839 it was founded by 33 Negroes who had been members of the first colored congregation in Buffalo. The church, which still stands at 511 Michigan Ave., was completed in 1845. In its deep basement and its pews many slaves found sanctuary while waiting for transportation to Canada.

There was a station on West Ferry Street near Niagara in a house which long has been gone from the scene.

The Court Street Hampton Dodge home was traditionally a station.

When the Morris Butler house at West Utica Street and Linwood Avenue was torn down in the 1920s, hiding places were found on either side of the front door, accessible only from the cellar. The house was built in 1857.

John Maxwell who lived on the old Two Mile Creek Road near the present Sheridan Drive, according to published recollections of his stepson, harbored slaves in his log house with a stone floor, warmed them before a big fireplace and got them to the Niagara by a short cut.

There are tales of escapes and rescues, of hired slave smugglers and professional slave catchers who operated along the Frontier.

A Negro, William Wells Brown, who worked on the Cleveland-Buffalo lake boat, hid many slaves on the ship and saw them safe to Canada—without price.

A German named Zeigler who lived at Black Rock had been a dresser in a playhouse in the Fatherland and was an expert at makeup. He once painted three Negroes white, disguised two of them as women and when their master came to claim them, he failed to recognize his chattels. The trio escaped.

One Benjamin Baker is credited with filling sleighs with grain under which slaves were hidden and driving them across on the ice to the Woodlawn grist mill at Great Mill Point, Ontario.

A free Negro living in Buffalo made a business of going South after wives of men who had escaped to Northern states or to Canada and was well paid for his services by abolitionists.

Samuel Murray, a free-born Negro, who came to Buffalo from Reading, Pa. in 1852, worked at the American Hotel. On his way to work he would be accosted by strange Negroes, asking: "Which way Canada?" Murray would go into the hotel, return with food for the fugitives and escort them out Niagara Street, seeing them aboard the ferry or other lake boats.

A Detroit Negro made money informing slave catchers of the whereabouts of runaways. Murray recalled that when word came that this traitor was coming to Buffalo, he was met by a "reception committee," which took him into a thicket, tied him to a tree, stripped him and cow-hided him into unconsciousness. He staggered back to the city and complained to police who locked up his assailants. A few days afterward they were quietly released. The betrayer of his own people was never again seen in Buffalo.

Two men once attempted to seize a Negro escapee on Niagara Street near West Ferry Street in Buffalo in daylight. The muscular fugitive fought savagely but was being overpowered by whips when abolitionists rushed to his rescue. The hunted Negro escaped in the melee.

In Niagara Falls, N.Y. a nearly white Negro named Sneedon was seized on a trumped-up murder charge, to get him back South. When he went on trial in Buffalo, abolitionists hired an able lawyer to defend him and he was acquitted. Soon he was spirited across the border.

On the north side of the Buffalo Historical Society's stately Museum in Delaware Park, a tablet depicts escaping Negroes being escorted to the Black Rock ferry.

It illustrates a significant chapter in the history of America and of Upstate New York—"Operation Underground."

Chapter 16

Southwest Passage

"To see a young boy roughly seized without process by armed men, manacled and smuggled away with no right to establish his freedom, if he is free, nor to offer evidence in self defense, appears to be perversion of the Common Law."

So commented the *Jamestown Journal* on the seizure at Busti in October, 1851, of a runaway slave, Harrison Williams, aged 17, who had been taken back South in irons by slave catchers.

Local law officers did not assist them and abolitionists made a futile attempt to rescue the youth. The incident was one of many which stirred Chautauqua County in the years which followed enactment of the hated Fugitive Slave Law.

The youth was one of seven fugitive Negroes who arrived at Busti, an underground station, southwest of Jamestown and near the state line, early in 1851.

The chief stationmaster at Busti was Squire Alvin Plumb. His aides were the Rev. John Broadhead, Levi Jones, Humphrey Pratt and William Storum, who was part Negro. Storum's daughter, Caroline, married the Rev. J. W. Loguen, a noted Underground leader at Syracuse who became a bishop of the African Methodist Episcopal Church.

All seven runaways were taken in by farmers in the neighborhood. They felt themselves to be so secure that they ventured into Jamestown that October of 1851 to see Dan Rice's Circus.

One of them, Sam Smith, came scurrying back to Busti to report that he had seen his former master on a street in Jamestown. Underground leaders sounded an alarm and all the fugitives were hidden in a swamp—except young Harrison Williams.

Levi Jones rode his horse at break-neck speed to the Storum farm to warn Williams but arrived too late. The slave hunters had come upon the youth milking a cow in the barnyard and seized him. They put him in irons and threw him in a carriage. Two other carriage loads of Southerners scoured the countryside for the other slaves, before they took Williams to Jamestown.

Jones tried to recruit a party to rescue the boy but could not muster enough volunteers. He and Silas Shearman of Jamestown followed the Southern party toward Fredonia but never caught up with it.

The other Negroes were spirited to Dunkirk and put on a boat which carried them across Lake Erie to Canada. The slavers followed in another boat but were too late.

So only Harrison Williams was taken back South into bondage. In 1864 James Broadhead, a Union soldier stationed near Culpepper, Va., met Harrison. He had been sold to a new master in Georgia and accompanied him to war as a body servant. Master and slave were both captured by Union troops at Gettysburg. The Negro was a hostler for Federal soldiers when his friend from Busti ran across him.

Jamestown was an early center of the abolition movement. In 1820 there were three slaves in the village. A few free Negroes lived in and around Jamestown.

In 1837 abolitionist lectures in the Baptist meeting house were stormed by mobs. At one meeting candles, candlesticks and snowballs were thrown at the speaker. The pastor was arrested for disturbing the peace, but was acquitted after trial.

Sentiment had changed by 1845 when a former slave addressed an anti-slavery convention without being disturbed.

After the Underground Railroad got under full steam, two main lines threaded Chautauqua County, although routes were often changed as circumstances warranted.

One route led from Oberlin and Painesville, Ohio, to Erie, Pa., to Westfield, Fredonia and Silver Creek, thence along Lake Erie to Buffalo and Black Rock on the Niagara.

The other ran from Warren, Pa. to Busti, Jamestown, Ellington, Cherry Creek, thence into Cattaraugus County through Leon, Dayton, Perrysburg and Versailles. It is said one fork swung westward from Leon to Forestville and Fredonia; the other led directly to the Niagara Frontier.

One Underground conductor was a justice of the peace and a deacon, others were physicians and one was a minister. Their names were never revealed because of the stiff penalties for violations of the Fugitive Slave Law.

Strange hideouts provided asylum for the escaped Negroes. Tradition has it that the belfries of the Sherman Presbyterian Church and of churches in Westfield were "stations." Remote barns also were often used, although there were shelters for the fugitives in several villages.

A leading Underground agent in Jamestown was Silas Shearman, whose old home at Pine and Fourth Streets was razed in 1910. He fed the slaves he hid in the haymow of his barn and collected funds to ship his charges on to the next station. Another Jamestown sanctuary was the home of Mrs. Catherine Harris on West Seventh Street.

There is a tradition that the Edward Work house in Falconer, now the site of a bank, was a station. Another reputed haven was the old Chicken Tavern, once a noted stop on the stage coach route between Jamestown and Silver Creek.

The homestead of Hiram Thayer at Frewsburg, another station, still stands. Thayer sheltered slaves overnight, then took them on to Silver Creek. The reputed operator at the Ellington station was Joseph B. Nessle.

Dr. James Pettit, a leader in the Underground movement, was the head station master at Fredonia, according to a booklet titled *The Underground Railroad in Southern Chautauqua County*, by William S. Bailey.

Doctor Pettit's son, Eber M., who ran a station at Versailles, Cattaraugus County, was one of the few Underground conductors to put his experiences in writing.

In *Sketches of the History of the Underground Railway*, a rare little book today, Eber Pettit included the adventures of an escaped Negro identified only as Dan.

It seems Dan had been sent from Corning to Dunkirk on a freight train which arrived in the Lake Erie port town in the evening. The agent to whom he was consigned bought Dan a ticket for Buffalo and put him behind a door at one end of a coach on a New York Central passenger train.

Just as the train started, two men took seats at the other end of the coach. Their backs were toward Dan, who recognized one of the men as his old master and the other as a much-feared slave catcher.

When the conductor asked Dan for his ticket, the frightened Negro asked him to "please stop the train and let me off." The shrewd conductor asked: "Are you afraid of those two fellows with red whiskers?" Dan allowed he was. But in reply to the conductor's question, he said he did not believe the two men had recognized him.

"Follow me," the conductor said. He led Dan into another coach and told him to step off the train when it reached Silver Creek. There he was to hide behind a woodpile until the train had left when the station agent would tell him where next to go. The railroad conductor was obviously in cahoots with the Underground operators.

Dan switched to the invisible railway and the Underground took him to Arkwright. His next stop was an UGRR station near Forestville where he was warmed, fed and hidden in an old house in a field. Eber Pettit was in charge of that part of the escape.

After the Underground people figured enough time had elapsed so that the coast was clear, Dan was taken to Black Rock, across the Niagara from Canada. There it was found spies were watching every boat leaving on a regular run.

So Dan's escort left his carriage on a back street and led the fugitive to the place where a row boat was hidden, out of the water. It was launched in a twinkling, and Dan and two boatmen were on their way to Canada before the alarm could be sounded.

Dan came back to Chautauqua County and worked in the area the next summer, attending school in the fall. After the outbreak of the Civil War he went to the front as an orderly for a Chautauqua county officer. He must have been a valuable piece of property. Otherwise his old master would not have gone to such great pains in his efforts to capture him.

Chapter 17

Tar and Feathers

More than one slave hunter rued the day he set foot in the old Cattaraugus County town of Olean on the Allegheny River.

For Olean had a well organized band of abolitionists and was a key center of Underground Railroad operations. The place was most unhospitable to strangers who came to town asking about fugitive Negroes. A few of these visitors got an Olean-made suit of tar and feathers.

In 1834, according to the reminiscences of James G. Johnson, a leading citizen, four stalwart young Negroes came to Martin's Hotel in Olean, asking for food and inquiring the route to Canada.

While the four were eating in the kitchen, two Virginia planters rode up on horseback, accompanied by a giant guide, "a gorilla type," mounted on a mule.

Innkeeper Martin told the Virginians that some Negroes had just left for Buffalo on the Allegany Road. The slave hunters dashed off in that direction. They were back in two hours—without any captives. Martin refused the Southerners lodging for the night and the rider of the mule got a thick coat of tar and feathers, applied in the Quirin lumber yard across Creek Bridge.

Meanwhile the hunted Negroes were safely hidden on

the property of Judge James Brooks in Pleasant Valley, north of Olean.

Another story involves three slaves hidden in the cellar of Henry Blake while the Southerner looking for them was getting the tar-and-feathers treatment among Judge Morton's piles of lumber. After the man had left town in great haste, the Negroes were disguised and shipped via the Underground to Canada. Not a capture of a runaway slave was ever recorded in Olean.

As early as 1825 the first Negroes began arriving in the river town. They were sent on the freedom road as soon as possible. At one time the Baptists maintained a Sunday-school for children of the slaves.

One who stayed in Olean was "Aunt Sarah" Johnson, a practical nurse who married Henry Johnson, a barber, lived in a house at South Fourth and West Green Streets and raised a large family. Her husband served with the Union forces in the Civil War.

Most of the fleeing Negroes came to Cattaraugus County from Pennsylvania by the water routes, particularly the Allegheny.

Three branches of the railroad without rails or locomotives ran across the county. One began at Buck Pond outside Olean where a Genesee Valley Canal boat was kept ready to take the fugitives up the Ischua Creek to Cadiz. There they stayed overnight at the Mead house, which, with its convenient outside cellarway, still stands. The next stop was Arcade.

A second route led from Olean to Pleasant Valley where Judge Brooks sheltered runaways in a building near his large house. The next stop was the Hatch or Hollis Scott place at Maplehurst, north of the village of Hinsdale. Then the blacks found asylum at the Isaac Searl or Burlingame home near Cadiz.

At that village the route split, one fork leading to Arcade, the other by back roads to the home of Joseph Remington on the Gooseneck Road, one mile east of Riceville in the Town of Ashford. Thence the trail led into Springville in Erie County and on to the Niagara Frontier.

Remington, a Vermonter, came to Riceville in 1835 and bought land on which he built a small shed with a loft. Eight children climbed the ladder which led to the loft bedroom. In 1839 Remington built the frame house where slaves were concealed in the cellar. The homestead has been modernized in recent years.

Joseph Remington was the great-grandfather of Miss Julia G. Pierce, Cattaraugus County historian to whom I am deeply indebted for digging up the Underground lore of the county in which both she and I were born.

According to stories handed down in her family, the escapees came to the Remington place after dark, usually only two or three at a time. They were fed and rested in the cellar until the next night.

Then they were loaded into a wagon or sleigh, hidden in straw or under blankets and taken to the next station, some 12 miles away.

The third route brought the slaves on Allegheny River boats to Quaker Bridge on the fringe of the Allegany Indian Reservation and near the present vast Allegany State Park. From Quaker Bridge, where in pioneer times the Friends had succored the neglected Indians and in a later day aided the Underground riders, the trail led to Leon, where it joined another link coming up from Chautauqua County. Thence it wound through Dayton, Perrysburg and Versailles.

In the isolated community of Versailles in the Town of Perrysburg and on the Cattaraugus Creek, close to Lake Erie, there were four reputed stations.

One was operated by Hiram Chapman, a retired sea captain who became a nurseryman and vegetable grower. Nearby was the home of Levi Palmen with a room on its second floor accessible only through a trap door and, according to tradition, the hiding place for the refugees.

On the crest of the second hill on Main Street in Versailles stood the Merrill place, said to have been another station. It burned down many years ago. Recently some boys found an unexplained recess in its cellar wall.

Also in Versailles was the well known station of Eber M. Pettit, who made medicine from formulas obtained from the Indians on the neighboring Cattaraugus Reservation and who wrote about his experiences as a conductor on the Underground Railroad.

It is believed that Negroes were boated down the Cattaraugus Creek, then much deeper and flowing more swiftly than today, the ten miles to Lake Erie.

Three runaway slaves, apparently from the same plantation, never got farther north than Versailles. George Washington Fitzpatrick and Mr. and Mrs. Thomas Jefferson Fitzpatrick are buried side by side in the North Cemetery there.

Chapter 18

Secret Journeys

Many a morning the children of William Sortore, a prosperous Allegany County farmer, would go to the barn to find the horses tired and dirty and the wagon or sleigh spattered with mud or snow. When they asked their father where the animals and vehicles had been, he refused to answer.

Sortore was equally secretive with his neighbors. Only a few fellow abolitionists knew that he ran a busy station of the Underground Railroad.

His big white farm house still stands on the "Back Road," between Scio and Belmont, about two miles south of the latter village, on the west side of the Genesee River.

Sortore once was in the employ of Philip Church, the master of Villa Belvidere, the estate on the river near Angelica. Rumors that the caretaker of the mansion hid slaves in the cellar of the mansion during Underground days have been discounted by modern researchers. The aristocratic Churches were not abolitionists.

Probably Sortore's station was linked with one at Friendship and the well-known haven operated in the hilltop village of Short Tract in the Town of Granger by the Rev. A. A. Richmond. Some villagers believe the preacher-stationmaster lived in the former Ethel Tuttle house;

others in the Loren Irish place. There also reputedly was a station in the Town of Hume. These Allegany County hideaways tied in with the Western New York UGRR routes which converged at the Niagara.

An early slave-holder in the Canisteo Valley was James McBurney, a Protestant Irishman who served as a colonel in the War of 1812, and who in 1797 built a fine frame mansion on a 1,600 acre estate on the Canisteo-Hornell Road. The building is said to be the oldest in Steuben County.

Ironically, a nephew of the colonel, Thomas Magee, is said to have operated a hideout for runaway Negroes on the same estate where his uncle had kept slaves. Presumably the runaways used the Canisteo River through the valley on their way to Canada.

Pitts Mansion in Honeoye, Another Refuge

SITE OF
UNDERGROUND
RAILROAD TERMINUS
HOME OF SAMUEL CUYLER USED
AS TERMINUS OF UNDERGROUND
R. R. DURING SLAVERY PERIOD.

Site of Cuyler Station at Pultneyville

Photo by Katherine Merrill

Chapter 19

The 4 A.M. Train

In the 1850s a northbound train used to pull out of Elmira regularly at 4 o'clock in the morning. It was in a sense a "Freedom Train," for its baggage car often carried, hidden among the trunks and piles of luggage, a few fugitive slaves. They were bound, nonstop, for the Canadian border and freedom.

They were there because of the Elmira station master of another "railroad," the invisible Underground line. That man was John W. Jones, a Negro born in slavery and one of Elmira's most remarkable citizens.

He was born in 1817 on a plantation near Leesburg, Va. The bright, likable boy was a favorite of his spinster mistress, although she never bothered to teach him to read and write.

In later years John Jones used to tell how one Spring day, when he was just a little fellow on the plantation and his grandmother was telling him stories, he saw a flock of wild geese winging north. He asked the old woman where the birds were going and she replied: "Up North where there is no slavery." He never forgot that remark. It planted in his mind the first impulse for freedom.

There came a time when his kindly mistress, old and ailing, could no longer manage her plantation and began hiring out her slaves. John Jones knew that—or being sold—would be his fate too. So on the night of June 3, 1844 he set out with two half brothers and two other slaves on a road that led toward the North Star and the place "where there is no slavery."

They stuffed their pockets with all the food they would hold. Each carried a pistol and a knife. John Jones had purloined his mistress's best carving knife. It was the only article he ever stole in his life. He had a few dollars, earned by doing extra work on another plantation.

Soon after entering Maryland, by daylight, they had a narrow escape. At a crossroads three slave catchers challenged them but the five runaways' display of armament and readiness to fight their way through scared the three man-hunters off.

The next day the actions of a lame man on a lame horse aroused their suspicions. This man would keep just ahead of the fugitives, stopping his horse and dismounting every few minutes. They figured he was keeping track of their movements and giving signals to someone.

Their suspicions were confirmed, for shortly a dozen men on horseback appeared in the distance, headed toward the five Negroes. The lame man had vanished. Jones and his comrades quickly scrambled up the side of a mountain. They were well up its steep slope when the horsemen reached its foot. The slave catchers did not choose to follow their quarry on foot and rode away.

The fugitives breathed easier after they crossed the Pennsylvania line and stood on free soil, but they pressed on night and day. It was July before the tired, hungry, desperate little group sought refuge at the South Creek farm of Dr. Nathaniel Smith near Elmira, across the New York state border.

The Smiths took compassion on them and harbored them for a week. Mrs. Smith fed them well. John Jones never forgot her kindness.

The fugitives finally ventured into the brisk canal port-railroad town of Elmira. Jones had a rare capacity for making friends and right away got work at odd jobs. He attracted the attention of Judge Ariel E. Thurston, who gave him employment as a caretaker in his sister's private seminary for girls. The judge also saw to it that the 27-year-old John went to another school and learned the three Rs.

At that time Elmira housed a few abolitionists, influential and determined citizens, who defied the majority of their fellow townspeople. And there were at least a dozen other fugitive Negroes in and around Elmira when Jones and his party arrived.

In 1846 some 40 members had been read out of the Presbyterian Church after they objected to the pastor's sermon in defense of slavery. The rebels formed an independent Congregational Church. Among them were the rich and socially-elect Jervis Langdons. Their daughter, Olivia, was to marry a drawling, gangling writer with red hair and a shaggy mustache. He was Samuel Langhorne Clemens, known to fame under his pen name, Mark Twain.

So when in 1850 the Fugitive Slave Law spurred the Underground Railroad into far-flung activity, the movement found strong sympathizers in the village near the state line.

Meanwhile Jones had married, been accepted by the community and given the job of sexton of the First Baptist Church. He moved into a yellow house near the church.

That dwelling was to house hundreds of fugitive slaves in the decade before the Civil War.

Jones quietly took command of the Underground in Elmira, a gateway between the South and the North. It became the principal station on the "railroad" between Philadelphia and the Canadian border. Jones worked closely with William Sill, the chief Underground agent in Philadelphia, who forwarded parties of from six to 10 fugitives at a time to Elmira.

In Pennsylvania the usual route led through Harrisburg, Williamsport, Canton and Alba. At Alba, 25 miles south of Elmira, the efficient station master was Charles G. Manley. From Elmira the Underground network forked off, north, northwest and northeast, but all the branches led to Canada.

Jones had many allies in Elmira. Mrs. John Culp, daughter of John Hendy, Elmira's first settler, hid runaways in her home. Other Underground leaders were the Langdons, Simeon Benjamin, the founder of Elmira College; Thomas Stanley Day, S. G. Andrus, John Slover, Riggs Watrous and others.

The station master concealed as many as 30 slaves at one time in his home, exactly where he never told. He carried on his operations so secretly that only the inner circle of abolitionists knew that in a decade he dispatched nearly 800 slaves to Canada.

John Jones demonstrated his winning ways in inducing the railroad baggagemen to stow away the hundreds of men, women and children who were spirited away to freedom.

In 1854 the railroad from Williamsport to Elmira was completed and Jones received many more fugitives by train, to ship away in the 4 o'clock "Freedom Baggage

Car," directly to Niagara Falls via Watkins Glen and Canandaigua, where the car was shifted to the New York Central. Most of Jones's "baggage" eventually landed in St. Catharines. The line from Pennsylvania through Elmira to Canandaigua became part of the Northern Central Railroad, long since taken over by the Pennsylvania system.

The year 1854 also brought to Elmira a valuable abolitionist ally in the Rev. Thomas K. Beecher, member of the famous family of divines, educators and authors. "Father Tom," who served in Elmira for more than 40 years, became pastor of the independent Congregational congregation which in 1875 changed its name to the Park Congregational Church. Its imposing edifice stands today facing Wisner Park and the First Baptist house of worship which John Jones served as sexton for 43 years.

Many slaves who did not ride the 4 o'clock "special" took an overland route out of Elmira through Hornell, Genesee County, Pembroke and Clarence to the Niagara. In the immediate Elmira area there was a station at Big Flats.

Abolitionists' efforts to rescue fugitives from slave catchers caused riots in Boston, Syracuse and other Northern cities. But in Elmira in 1858 there was a near riot over a slave who wanted to return to bondage.

An old Negro who had escaped via the Underground found himself in Canada, crippled by rheumatism and unable to provide for himself. He yearned for "Ol' Massa" and the old plantation in Calvert County, Maryland. So he wrote his owner, John W. Mills, to come to Canada and take him back "home."

Mills traveled to Canada and, accompanied by the Negro, stopped in Elmira on their way back to Maryland. The word got around that a slave catcher was in town with a captured fugitive. A crowd of Negroes, armed with knives and pistols, surrounded the pair, determined on a rescue. The old slave tried to explain the true facts. The mob would not listen and finally Mills and the Negro got away by running for the train which took them back South.

John Jones did not figure in that incident but at another time when a Negro from Buffalo, misrepresenting himself as a fugitive, began collecting money in Elmira, the usually mild-mannered Jones almost literally kicked the impostor out of town.

After the Civil War burst upon the land, the Elmira Underground station virtually ceased to exist. Instead the town became a reception and training center for Union troops. Later it housed a prison for captured Confederate soldiers.

In 1859 Jones had taken over the duties of sexton of Elmira's Woodlawn Cemetery. During the war he buried nearly 3,000 Rebel prisoners. He saw to it that in every plain pine coffin was placed a sealed bottle, telling the name, rank, company, regiment, date of death and grave number of every Confederate.

At the head of every grave was a wooden slab with a number on it. Sexton Jones wrote down every record in a book. In 1877 the federal government took over the Confederate burial plot and made Woodlawn a national cemetery. The wooden markers were replaced with identical headstones.

Many a family in the old slave-holding South owes a lasting debt to a former slave. For the records Jones kept so carefully were taken to Washington where a drawing was made, showing every grave and number. Relatives of the Southern dead still visit the Elmira cemetery seeking out the graves of their ancestors who died in a Northern prison.

Jones was paid $2.50 for each burial. At the end of the war he was able to buy a farm on College Avenue, where he died in 1900 at the age of 83.

For years visitors to Woodlawn noticed there were always fresh flowers on the grave of Mrs. Nathaniel Smith. She was the first to befriend John Jones and his fellow fugitives when first they came to the Elmira area in 1844. Only after Jones was laid to rest in the cemetery he had tended so long did it become known that his hand had put the flowers there.

Chapter 20

Around the Lakes

Ithaca, nestling among the great hills of the scenic Central New York Lakes Country, was a Mecca for slaves traveling the Underground as early as the 1830s. It had a militant anti-slavery society. It also had its share of conservatives.

The Quakers were active in the abolition cause and their brethren in Philadelphia sent on many runaway slaves to the Friends in Tompkins County.

The usual Underground route into Ithaca was via Montrose, Pa. and Owego. A number of Negro fugitives remained in the area, even after the stampede to Canada in the wake of the passage of the Fugitive Slave Law.

Many of the runaways were welcomed in Ithaca by barber George Johnson, a free-born Negro. He would obtain cash and clothing for them from a leading lawyer of the town, Ben Johnson, and speed them on toward Canada. His helpers were Benjamin Halsey, John Murdock and E. T. Tillotson.

Three routes led out of Ithaca. All converged at the foot of Cayuga Lake where they joined the main trail which ran through Auburn and Syracuse, thence to Oswego and other border ports.

One route was by Cayuga Lake steamboat, usually the

good ship *Simeon DeWitt,* which took them to the famed long wooden Cayuga Bridge.

Another freedom road led overland to Ludlowville on the east side of Cayuga Lake, then inland to Sherwood and Auburn.

A third Underground line followed the west shore of Cayuga Lake to Trumansburg, Covert, Farmer (Interlaken) and on to the foot of the lake.

From Eastern points in Tompkins County the most direct route was through Cortland and Homer to Syracuse.

Among the several Underground stations in and around Ithaca, one of the most unusual was the Congregational chapel built at Trumansburg by Charles Hayt, after he had been kicked out of the Ithaca Presbyterian Church for his abolitionist sympathies. And he had been a trustee of the Ithaca church. Hayt and Deacon Luce cared for sick and infirm fugitives at their Trumansburg haven.

The building which later housed the Wortman meat market in Ithaca is said to have harbored a dozen Negroes in its cellar at one time.

A stout-hearted abolitionist was Alexander Murdock, a Scot, who despite threats that his home would be burned, continued to shelter slaves. Mrs. Edith Scott of Giles Street was credited with leading runaways to the shore of Cayuga Lake, to be rowed across the lake to a station linked with the main line.

In the 1850s Thomas Jackson, a Negro employed by tanner Edward Estey, paid one of his race $50 to have his mother brought to Ithaca from the South.

A prominent Ithaca banker, Joseph B. Williams, in 1858 was one of the promoters of a unique scheme for liberating the slaves. It had nothing to do with the Underground, except to serve as a footnote to the history of the anti-slavery movement.

Williams was vice president of the National Emancipation Society which conceived the idea of using the proceeds from the sale of public lands to buy the slaves their freedom. The movement never got beyond the idea stage.

In Tompkins County outside the Ithaca limits were several known Underground stations. Linked to the one operated by Ben Joy at Ludlowville is a strange tale.

One day a young employe of Joy's worked in the field until twilight. Returning to the barn, he went up into the haymow to throw down some feed for the team of horses he had just unhitched.

When he plunged his fork into the hay, he was startled by piercing screams of pain and a voice pleading for mercy. The outcries, which startled the neighborhood, came from a male Negro who had been stabbed by the fork tines. Ben Joy, little thinking his hired man would be feeding the horses at 9 P.M., had hidden the Negro in the mow. The slave was not seriously wounded and was able to get on to the next station within a day.

The Ludlows, who gave their name to the lakeside community, also are said to have sheltered fugitives.

One day in 1856 abolitionist Chauncey Douglas, who lived near East Lansing, heard in Ithaca about a slave who had wandered into the town and was being hunted. Douglas found the runaway, took him to his home just west of the East Lansing church, got a fresh team and drove the Negro to Auburn, only a few hours ahead of the slave hunters.

Horace Cooper, who ran the Farmers Inn at Jacksonville, took in fugitive slaves. In later years Hezekiah Van Order told how when he was a boy of about 10 years he saw a Negro woman come to the inn, leading a young boy and carrying a baby. They were sheltered for the night. A few days later a slave catcher came to the inn looking for the trio. Another refugee at the inn was a Negro chimneysweep who showed his gratitude by cleaning the hotel's chimneys before he pushed on toward freedom.

The Groton-Dryden area northeast of Ithaca was dotted with slave havens. Part of the old house in Peruville off Route 38, where Henry Teeter and his wife harbored fugitives, is still standing. The Teeters' old dog, Major, was a valued assistant, for he would bark furiously whenever a stranger approached the station.

Historical markers designating them as onetime Underground stations stand in front of two houses a quarter of a mile apart on the Lower Creek Road at Etna.

One station, a small, weather-beaten frame house, was operated by Hananiah Wilcox and his wife, Nancy, who sent slaves on to the next station, presumably Cortland.

The other is a handsome white house, greatly altered over the years. There abolitionists William Hanford and his wife, Altha, gave asylum to runaway slaves. The place until recent years was in the hands of Hanford's descendants.

The old Pritchard place in Ringwood, Town of Dryden, has recently yielded evidence of having been a hideout. When a new owner was remodeling the house, he uncovered a secret cellar. In it, under a pile of shavings, nearly 30 pairs of leather boots were found. Maybe they were hidden there for the use of slaves who changed their footgear in their northward flight. But that is in the realm of conjecture.

In the early years Southerners came to the Town of Caroline and set up a considerable slave colony. There were as many as 32 bondsmen in the area at one time. The Speeds of Virginia, the Boices, the Hydes, the Petillos and others lived in true plantation style. A leader in the migration from the South was Dr. James Speed, whose plantation home, Spring Farm, was on the Old Level Green Road, near Route 79. Nearby is an old slave burying ground with 14 unmarked graves.

A kinsman, John James Speed, who had bought and sold slaves in Virginia, brought four of his Negroes with him to Caroline in 1805. One of them was Peter Webb, then aged 13.

In 1811 Peter and his master made an agreement. Peter was to be permitted to buy his freedom with $350 plus $50 interest. He was to work outside the plantation to earn his "ransom" money. For seven years the young Negro worked on farms, in mills and as a hostler until he had saved the sum needed to buy his release. In December, 1818, he paid John Speed $400 and became a free man.

The former slave bought a farm, raised a family and was one of the founders of the African Methodist Church in Ithaca. His unusual story is told in a brochure titled *Peter Webb, Slave-Freeman-Citizen* by Sydney Gallwey, a talented Negro teacher who has been making a comprehensive study of the history of his people in the region.

Many of the fugitives who left the Ithaca area for Canada settled at Dawn Mills in Kent County, Province of Ontario. Some of them returned to spend the rest of their days after the Civil War in the old town at the head of Cayuga Lake.

In the Mecklenburg area just over the Tompkins County line in Schuyler County, Parker Wixom and some Quaker families were operatives of the invisible railway. Wixom is said to have concealed slaves in a tiny room under a back kitchen door. After his charges had rested overnight, he would drive them the next evening to the nearest station near Lodi, Seneca County.

Joseph McKee, a prosperous Quaker farmer, was the stationmaster at the old village of Steamburg in the Town of Hector on Seneca Lake in Schuyler County.

An historical marker stands in front of the low white house with wide porches on the Erway farm at Gabriel's Junction near the union of Routes 14 and 14-A, four miles north of Watkins Glen. The legend on it reads: "Underground Railroad. Luther Cleveland and his wife sheltered fugitive slaves here and helped them on their way to Canada."

Cleveland was an elder in the Pioneer Presbyterian Church of Reading. According to local tradition, he hid slaves in his cellar which was divided into several rooms. Long ago the partitions were torn down.

Another station was reputedly operated by Luther Myers who lived on a dirt road in what is now the Watkins Glen State Park. He ran a mill which was powered by the stream that raced down the rocky mountainside.

The miller's daughter, the late Alice Myers Cowing, recalled that in her childhood she would hear light knocks at the back door and hear strange voices in the Myers home. She recalled coming down stairs one night to find her parents treating the lacerated shoulder of a Negro who presumably had been bitten by a dog. Her parents swore her to secrecy about these incidents and only after they were long dead did she reveal them.

Two decades before the Underground Railroad got up a full head of steam, slave catching was unpopular—and was resisted—in Yates County.

One summer day in 1830 residents of Eddytown, now

Lakemont, in the Town of Starkey, were startled to see a group of horsemen galloping through their quiet village. Excitement mounted when it was learned that two of the riders were Virginia planters hot on the trail of seven runaway slaves. A few local men who had no scruples about how they made a dollar had been induced to join in the search.

There were some staunch abolitionists in the town on the eastern shore of Lake Seneca. Three of them, Isaac Lanning, Patrick Quinn and Abner Chase, knew the whereabouts of the hunted Negroes and rode off to warn them. They were too late.

Four of the seven fugitives had been rounded up and manacled. Three had been seized at work in the harvest on Zenas Kelsey's farm. The fourth was taken at the Red Mill.

The abolitionists put up a bold front. Lanning told the slavers: "You shall not take those men back." The Southerners allowed they would do just that. When farmer Kelsey showed signs of fight, one of the planters drew his sword. Lanning stepped between the pair. In firm tones he told the Virginians they would have to prove their claim to the slaves in court.

Meanwhile Lanning had sent a young neighbor on his own fleet horse to warn the three other fugitives. When the youth found the trio mowing hay for Silas Spink at Milo, he gave them this message from Lanning: "Go to Mr. Bradley at Penn Yan and he will tell you what to do."

Walter Wolcott, in recounting the incident in his *Military History of Yates County,* did not further identify "Mr. Bradley" but it is safe to conclude he was an abolitionist and, as events proved, an efficient operator.

News of the seizure of the four Negroes caused a near riot. Nearly 200 men milled about the tavern in which the

132

prisoners had been locked and were under guard. Some hotheads in the crowd wanted to free the slaves by force. James Taylor, who had been Yates County's first district attorney, restored calm by an eloquent appeal against violence, urging that the law be allowed to take its course.

At a hearing the next day before Peace Justice Isaac Seymour, the planters produced papers establishing their title to the slaves and the court ruled they could take their property.

But three Negroes were still at large. Their owners carried on the hunt for days. They were given several false leads, one that sent them on a futile journey to Rochester. The fugitives were never caught.

So after filing a suit for heavy damages against farmer Spink, a case which never came to trial, the two planters headed South with the four Negroes. But only one master and three slaves ever reached Virginia. One owner and one slave were taken ill in Elmira and died there.

While the Starkey manhunt was not a major incident in history, it showed that 30 years before the Civil War the idea of human bondage was abhorrent to many Yates County people.

As in many other Upstate communities the clashing opinions over the slavery issue was reflected in the churches of the shire town, Penn Yan. In 1841 Presbyterian abolitionists formed a Congregational church and dissident Methodists joined the Wesleyans.

Penn Yan lay on the Underground route which led from Watkins to Canandaigua and thence to the Lake Ontario ports. But it is not possible definitely to locate any stations that operated in the village. There is a tradition that the cellar of the large Sheppard house on Genesee Street had a section, long boarded up, which once housed fugitive slaves. Morris F. Sheppard and his son, Charles, are listed by Historian Wolcott as local anti-slavery leaders, along with Myron Hamlin, Samuel F. Curtis and Joseph Elmendorf.

Penn Yan also was on the Elmira & Canandaigua Railroad, now a part of the Pennsylvania system, and the story goes that in the 1850s when a certain northbound train stopped in the village slaves were put in baggage cars, joining other stowaways from Elmira. They were bound for the Niagara Frontier, so close to Canada and freedom.

In 1830 Julius Bull built a noble cobblestone house on his 246-acre farm on the western shore of Cayuga Lake about one mile south of Bridgeport.

Bull, a big, powerful man of cultivated tastes, was an ardent supporter of the anti-slavery cause and his home, known locally as "The Cobblestone," was reputedly a station of the Underground.

It lay across Cayuga Lake from Union Springs, which had a large Quaker population, and it is believed that fugitive slaves were brought across the lake to Bull's place in boats.

A tale has been handed down that one day, just as a train was pulling into Seneca Falls, Julius Bull drove up in a carriage with a Negro in its back seat. Just as the men who were hunting the fugitive stepped off the train, Bull quickly shoved the slave into the baggage car, then mingled with the crowd to allay suspicion. The Negro escaped.

Seneca County Sheriff G. Kenneth Wayne, a great-grandson of William G. Wayne, who bought the Bull farm in the mid 1870s, recalls as a young boy playing in the attic of the house and seeing straw-covered wooden bunks on which the fugitives supposedly slept. The windowless attic was accessible by a trap door.

"The Cobblestone" was remodeled in the 1920s. It now is the home of Mr. and Mrs. Carleton Caulkins.

Chapter 21

"The Jerry Rescue"

On the night of Oct. 1, 1851 clouds hid the face of the moon and a great storm raged in Syracuse's Clinton Square. Nature did not spawn the storm. It came from the hearts of men.

That night 2,500 people milled about the Square. Some of them were there just to see a show. But most of them had come to defy the law and to release by force an obscure Negro from the brick police station at the south end of the Clinton Street bridge.

The Negro, a mulatto known as Jerry, in manacles and guarded by United States marshals, faced return to bondage in Missouri under the year-old Fugitive Slave Law. In the Square that October night were most of the abolitionists of Syracuse, their ranks swollen by delegates to the Liberty Party's state convention in session at the Congregational Church.

Jerry's legal name was William McHenry. That was the name of the prominent Missourian on whose plantation Jerry had been born some 37 years before. The slave was certain his master also was his father. He had been given an education, learned to keep his master's books and was a trusted servant. Yet he wanted freedom more than security. One day he fled across the line into free soil.

He found his way to Syracuse in 1849 and obtained work

in the cabinet shop of Charles F. Williston, a future mayor of the city. Jerry was strong, willing and personable. The next year he changed jobs and began making barrels for the salt works in a downtown cooper shop. He was in the shop alone the noon of Oct. 1 when the federal men came and arrested him on a trumped-up charge of theft.

Thus began the incident which went into the history books as "The Jerry Rescue."

It had been foretold 18 weeks earlier by none other then the great Daniel Webster. The Senator, speaking in Syracuse City Hall, defended the Fugitive Slave Law which he had helped to conceive. He denounced those who "set themselves above the law and the decisions of the highest tribunals" as "guilty of treason." And he declared, knowing full well that Syracuse was a hotbed of abolitionism:

"Depend on it, the law will be executed in all its spirit and to the letter. It will be executed in all the great cities— here in Syracuse, in the midst of the next anti-slavery convention if the occasion shall arise."

The convention met; the occasion arose, made to order with the arrest of Jerry. The abolitionists were not unprepared.

The four marshals who had seized the Negro in the cooper shop marched him to the office of U.S. Commissioner Sabine in the Townsend Block for arraignment as a fugitive slave. As Jerry entered the commissioner's office, some 40 men suddenly appeared and followed him in. In a minute the place erupted with swinging fists and flying furniture. A flying wedge opened a path for Jerry, blocked the way against the officials.

The Negro fled down the street, dodging among piles of cord wood brought in by farmers for sale. He was overtaken and overpowered after a four-block chase. He put up a stout fight before, his clothes torn, his face bloodied and a rib broken, he was thrown into a commandeered wagon. With one officer sitting on his chest and another on his legs, he was hauled to the office of Police Justice House at the corner of Clinton and West Water Streets.

Stones began raining on the police office windows and the court adjourned the case until the next morning. Jerry was put in a back room, in irons and under guard.

Meanwhile abolitionist leaders, among them the famous liberal clergyman, Dr. Samuel J. May, held a council of war in the Warren Street office of Dr. Hiram Hoyt. They had the guidance also of Gerrit Smith of Peterboro, in town for the Liberty Party convention.

Soon after 8 o'clock men armed with clubs, axes, stove wood and iron rods converged on Clinton Square. Their orders were to "avoid personal violence if possible, to press upon the officers, overwhelm them by numbers, not by blows."

Nevertheless there was violence and blows were struck. After smashing the doors and windows of the police office, the liberators swarmed in. They turned off the gaslights and battered down the wall of the back room where Jerry was confined. The outnumbered marshals bolted after firing two wild shots. One of the officers jumped out a window into the Erie Canal and emerged, dripping but unhurt. An imported deputy marshal, Henry Fitch, went back to Rochester with a broken arm.

In the confusion Jerry was pushed into the street and into a carriage where two men waited. His pursuers were given the slip as the carriage wound in and out of darkened streets, until it stopped at the home of Caleb Davis at Genesee and Orange Streets.

There for five days, while roads out of Syracuse were

watched and extra police searched the city, Jerry was safely hidden, his injuries cared for and new clothing provided.

In the darkness of the fifth night, a covered wagon drew up before the Davis house. Into it was helped a seemingly feeble old man. The get-away was a success. Jerry was rushed over the Underground route to the station at Mexico. His next stop was the farm of Sydney Clarke near Oswego.

There passage to Canada was arranged with a lake boat captain and another night found Jerry being rowed out to the schooner which took him across Lake Ontario to Kingston in Canada. Thence he went to St. Catharines, where a Syracuse friend set him up in a cabinet shop. Two years later Jerry died. He is buried in St. Catharines.

"The Jerry Rescue" had its inevitable aftermath in Syracuse. His liberators had faced the pistols of the marshals. Now they faced the law with the threat of fines and imprisonment.

On Oct. 15 eight men were arrested and 10 others indicted for violation of the Fugitive Slave Law. On Nov. 5 five more indictments were returned. Late in November there were four more arrests.

Of those arrested, only one, Enoch Reed, a Negro, was convicted. He died while his appeal was pending. One man was acquitted after trial. Juries disagreed in two other cases. The rest were repeatedly adjourned until they were dropped from the calendar.

Although Dr. May, Gerrit Smith and Syracuse abolitionist Charles A. Wheaton acknowledged in a newspaper statement that they had taken part in the "Jerry Rescue," they were not among those arrested.

Although shortly after the rescue, a Syracuse meeting voiced approval of the abolitionists' action, the majority of public sentiment was against them.

That feeling was expressed in a call issued for another mass meeting in Syracuse City Hall, on Oct. 25, directed to:

". . . the citizens of Syracuse and the County of Onondaga who are in favor of sustaining the Constitution and the laws of the country and who are desirous of expressing their abhorrence and reprobation of the late infamous proceedings in this city by which the laws have been violated, the government temporarily subverted and disgrace fixed upon the town in which these lawless acts were perpetrated."

More than 650 persons signed the call. Among them were some of the leading business and professional men of the community. There also were a few immigrants and laborers who saw their jobs threatened by liberated Negroes. Signers also included hotel men and saloonkeepers who resented the abolitionists' sympathy with the temperance movement.

Still the call and the big meeting clearly indicated the indignation of a large and influential segment of the community against abolitionists who took the law in their own hands. And Syracuse was considered a "liberal" town.

History has reversed the verdict of 1851. Today Syracuse counts among its finest hours "the late infamous proceedings," with its "lawless acts" which "disgraced" the city.

Dr. Alfred Mercer, Syracuse physician who died in 1914, made this provision in his will:

"To keep green the heroism of the men who rescued Jerry . . . I give $600 to the Onondaga Historical Association to be known as the Jerry Rescue Fund; the interest of which shall be used every five years to procure some person to deliver a Jerry Rescue oration on Oct. 1."

The Alfred Mercer Fund is still extant and used occasionally for an oration when some significant event warrants it. The last lecture was delivered on Oct. 1, 1951.

And a tablet on a building on Clinton Square marks the site of "the Jerry Rescue." It was put there in 1914 by Mrs. Lizzie Maynard, then owner of the block, at the request of Merriam Camp, Sons of Union Veterans. Some historians doubt that the building is the old police office which the abolitionists stormed in 1851. If it is, they maintain, its architecture indicates it has been altered beyond recognition.

Be that as it may, "the Jerry Rescue" lives in history as one of the most dramatic events in the long fight for freedom which culminated in the Emancipation Proclamation.

Twenty years before the celebrated "Jerry Rescue," the abolitionists of Syracuse helped another slave to freedom. "Harriet's Escape" did not arouse wide public clamor, it was not marked by mob violence, but it had its elements of drama.

In the early Fall of 1830, John Davenport, a Virignia planter, put up at the Syracuse House with his wife, baby and slave girl. Harriet Powell was an attractive, well-formed girl with a complexion as fair as that of her owners, the result, no doubt, of a white master's visit to a slave cabin.

When employes at the hotel discovered Harriet was a slave, not a white servant or a kinswoman of the Davenports, they went to the abolitionists and propsed her escape. A plot was quickly hatched. At first Harriet hung back. The Davenports treated her well and she knew that if the escape failed, she would be sold "down the river."

Finally she yielded to the persuasion of Deputy County Clerk William M. Clarke and John R. Owen, a marble dealer, who fashioned the escape strategy, with the help of a Negro waiter at the hotel.

The Davenports were to leave for the South on Oct. 8. The conspirators decided to spirit Harriet away on the night of Oct. 7. While a farewell party was being held for the Davenports in the hotel that night, Harriet was upstairs tending the baby.

Throwing a shawl over her shoulders, Harriet picked up the baby and went downstairs to the banquet hall. On the pretext she had to go out for a few minutes on an errand, she asked the mother to hold the child until she returned. Then she walked slowly to the rear door of the hotel—and the flight had begun.

A Negro escorted her to a carriage where Clarke and Owen were waiting. There was a brief halt at the Congregational Church where the abolitionists were meeting. Clarke passed the hat for money with which "to ship a stolen bale of goods."

Although it may not have been known by that name in 1830, the Underground was working efficiently. The first stop for Harriet was the home of an abolitionist named Sheppard at Marcellus. Next was Peterboro, the home of the rich and fanatical abolition leader, Gerrit Smith.

Meanwhile back in the Syracuse House, after Harriet had failed to return in 10 minutes, the planter and his wife sounded the alarm. Authorities searched the homes of known abolitionists. The Oswego-bound canal packet was ransacked in the frenzied search.

Davenport had handbills circulated, advertising a $200 reward for Harriet's return. They described her as "about five feet four, of a full, well proportioned form, with straight brown hair, dark eyes, of fresh complexion and so fair she generally would be taken for white."

She was not caught. Gerrit Smith got her to Canada via the Underground.

A year after her escape, planter Davenport went broke and all his property was sold under the hammer. Had Harriet Powell not accepted the assistance of freedom-loving people in a Northern village, she would have stood on the auction block in Dixie.

These dramatic events serve as footnotes to the long story of Syracuse's consistent struggle against the slavery forces. The Salt City for years was a center of the abolition movement.

It also was an important link of the Underground line which ran from Elmira to Oswego, Cape Vincent and other ports accessible to the free shores of Canada.

In October, 1850, not long after the adoption of the Fugitive Slave Law, a vigilance committee, one of the first in the nation, was formed in Syracuse's City Hall.

A leader in that group and one of the chief "conspirators" in "the Jerry Rescue" was the Rev. Dr. May, a Unitarian minister who came to Syracuse from Connecticut in 1845. In New England he had stumped for emancipation and was active in the temperance and woman's rights movements. He had been stoned by mobs and hanged in effigy for espousing unorthodox causes.

In Syracuse he became a mainstay of the Underground and harbored many slaves in his home before sending them on to freedom.

Dr. May presided at the rally of abolitionists held in Syracuse on the day that John Brown was executed and which adopted a resolution which declared that "John Brown is the heaven-sent protest against the despotism of of slavery."

This fearless and aggressive reformer was minister of the Church of the Messiah in Syracuse until his health failed in 1868. He died in 1871, after living to see the "despotism of slavery" crushed and the slaves emancipated.

Another key figure in the Syracuse Underground operation was the Rev. J. W. Luguen, a Negro preacher. He was the local station master and fitted up rooms in his home for escaped slaves. He was to write that he never turned a fugitive away from his door but a few who came were so filthy and bedraggled that he had to put them in the stable.

An influential friend of the Underground was a director of a visible railroad, the New York Central. He was Horace White, one of Syracuse's leading citizens, and he furnished fugitive slaves with passes on the Central's trains.

Only after his father's death, did Andrew D. White, who became the first president of Cornell University, learn of his sire's Underground activities. An aged Syracuse abolitionist told Andrew White he had often gone to the White home at night and rattled the windows to get the railroad director's attention.

Horace White would raise the window, ask how many passes were needed, sign the required number and pass them out the window to the Underground agent.

There were several stations in and around Syracuse. An important stop on the route to Oswego was Mexico. To the southeast of Syracuse was Auburn, the home of the famous Harriet Tubman, Seward and many other friends of the cause.

And in the lakeside village of Skaneateles the Evergreen House still stands at 98 West Genesee Street. It is a stately white colonial-type home with green blinds to match the evergreen trees and hedge that surround it. In Underground days it was known as the Fuller place and it is said that runaway Negroes were hidden in its cellar.

Chapter 22

The Jumping Off Place

It was not by chance that the "Jerry" of the celebrated Syracuse rescue, which is narrated in another chapter, escaped to Canada via Oswego.

For the historic lakeport was a jumping-off place for countless Canada-bound runaway slaves. Its location was strategic. Just across the blue-green waters of Lake Ontario lay the friendly Canadian haven of Kingston. And coastwise ships ran to Lewiston, principal Niagara gateway to the Negroes' "Promised Land."

A prime figure in the "Jerry Rescue" was the wealthy, fanatical, prophet-bearded Gerrit Smith of Peterboro, a national leader of abolition and one of the masterminds of the Underground Railroad.

He had a hand in choosing the Oswego escape route for "Jerry." For Gerrit Smith, although he never lived in Oswego, was the town's principal property owner. He controlled the Oswego Hydraulic Canal and the Pier and Dock Co. He donated a library to the community.

Oswego had a key place in his abolitionist interests, too. From his Madison County home, one of the busiest relay stations on the UGRR, he sent on to Oswego many of the hundreds of fugitive slaves he sheltered at Peterboro.

At Oswego he had a corps of trusted abolitionists and

his right-hand man in all his enterprises was his business agent and confidant, John B. Edwards.

Edwards, who in his youth had been a canaler at Lyons, came to Oswego to help build the Hydraulic and boat canals. In 1831 at the age of 30 he became Smith's land agent and manager of the Hydraulic Canal. He also handled "shipments" on the Underground Railroad.

Some of Edwards's letters to his employer bearing on the UGRR were quoted in an article in the *New York Folklore Quarterly* by Charles McCool Snyder, Oswego educator-historian.

In 1847 Edwards wrote: "That slavery-maimed and branded man, Robert Thompson, called on me with his subscription book and letters. . . . I raised $31.25 in this place and put him on a steamboat for Lewiston." He added that Smith had promised to provide a small house for the fugitive's family, expected to arrive in Oswego soon.

Smith donated homes to many Negroes in the village. After the enactment of the Fugitive Slave Law, some of them fled to Canada. Some of them returned—to dwell in the houses Smith had given them.

Edwards in 1854 wrote Smith that he had put 10 runaways, five women and five children, on a steamboat headed for Canada. He put up Fred Douglass in his home when the Negro leader came to speak in Oswego. In general, his correspondence with Smith contained few references to the Underground and they were understandably guarded ones.

John Edwards became a banker and business man in his own right. But when he died at the age of 95, he still was in the employ of the Smith family, although the old reformer had passed to his reward 20 years earlier. Edwards may have housed slaves in the East Third Street home he occupied during the Underground period, but there is no record of it.

Another influential abolitionist was lawyer James Brown, a leader in the Liberty party, who died just before the Civil War while on a trip to England. His former mansion, built of brick and in Federal style, still stands in East Oneida Street, shorn of its stately pillars and balcony. In her old age his widow told of a secret closet in her old home where runaway slaves were hidden. There is also the inevitable and unverified story of an underground passage leading from the house.

A tower of strength in the movement was the rich lumber dealer, Hamilton Littlefield. He owned his own ships, which were manned by Canadian sailors, and which transported fugitive blacks, as well as lumber, to Canada. He was a close friend of Gerrit Smith and the old Littlefield house at East Fourth and Oneida Streets is said to have been a refuge for escaping slaves.

Another abolitionist and Smith associate was the patrician George H. McWhorter. He lived in an 1830 stone Georgian house on East Mohawk Street but it is questionable that this man of conservative tastes ever turned it into an Underground station.

There is no question about the Underground activities of the Clarke brothers, Edwin W. and Sidney, sons of Oswego's first physician. Both figured in the "Jerry Rescue" story.

From the home of Edwin Clarke, a lawyer, who lived on East Mohawk Street, the fugitives were passed on to the farm of brother Sidney, east of the village and not far from the lake.

After "Jerry" had escaped from Syracuse, Ames, the Underground agent at Mexico, sent the much-sought fugitive on to the Clarkes in Oswego and he stayed four days at Sidney's farm before he was slipped to freedom on a lake boat.

"Jerry" was only one of an estimated 80 to 100 slaves who were concealed in and around the Clarke barn during the height of the Underground operation.

When the coast was clear, and darkness had fallen, Sidney would march his runaways to the docks. Occasionally he took them, hidden in a wagon load of straw. Transportation had been arranged with ship captains, most of whom were friendly to the cause. Some carried the Negroes for $1 a head. Other skippers charged nothing.

John J. Clarke, son of Sidney, recounting in 1931 stories of the Underground told him by his mother, wrote that slave hunters often searched the farm for Negro runaways— but never found any. On one occasion a timely warning from lawyer Edwin sent a batch of fugitives to safety in the woods back of the famous barn.

Travelers in the aptly-named Fruit Valley just southwest of Oswego notice a New York State Historical Society marker which reads:

"Site of Underground station, Edwards residence, 1860– 1865. Slaves transfered from here to homestead."

Local research has disclosed that John B. Edwards never lived there nor anyone else of that name. The Pease family lived in the homestead at the site of the marker and there is a tradition the Peases were connected with the Underground. There is no clue to the "homestead" reference on the sign and the Edwards connection is clearly erroneous.

When the State Historical Society show its slips in its markers, it's no wonder the trail of the invisible railway is so hard to follow. The last I knew the "Edwards" marker is still there.

About a station maintained at Fair Haven in Oswego County within sight of Lake Ontario and operated by a farmer named French, hangs a weird tale. Somehow a runaway Negro named Moses reached the French place. Along the line somebody had told the poor chap that abolitionists ate Negroes.

When the friendly French told the Negro he was an abolitionist and would help him to freedom, the frightened slave started to run. French had a hard time convincing Moses that abolitionists were not cannibalistic.

Chapter 23

Lincoln's Beard

No face is so deeply etched on the American mind as that of Abraham Lincoln. Even the tots recognize the lined countenance with the sad, inscrutable eyes—and the whiskers.

Maybe it is because of the whiskers. The Civil War President and his whiskers seem as inseparable as Teddy Roosevelt and his teeth, as Dwight Eisenhower and his grin, as Douglas MacArthur and his corncob pipe.

Lincoln was our first bearded President. But when he was elected in 1860 he was smooth-shaven. When he left Springfield for his first inaugural in 1861, a new crop of whiskers had sprouted on his chin.

Back of that hirsute adornment is a story in which a young Western New York girl played a leading role.

During the campaign of 1860 Grace Bedell was an 11-year-old school girl in Westfield, Chautauqua County. The village was plastered with pictures of the candidates and Grace was attracted to the Republican nominee. She had four older brothers and two of them were ardent Douglas Democrats.

There were lively arguments around the Bedell fireside when the Democratic brothers teased Grace by comparing

150

Human Chain Winds over Klondike Pass

A "Sourdough" and Friend

the homely Lincoln with the more handsome Stephen A. Douglas.

Grace studied the face on the Lincoln posters. She admired the noble brow and the fine eyes but the lower area of the angular features, with the deeply chiseled lines about the mouth, disturbed her. An idea came to her and she told her mother:

"I think Mr. Lincoln should grow a beard and I am going to write to him and tell him so."

On Oct. 15, with the election drawing near, Grace sat down and carefully wrote in pencil this letter:

Hon. A. B. Lincoln,
Dear Sir:

My father has just come from the fair and brought home your picture and Mr. Hamlin's. I am a little girl only eleven years old but want you should be President of the United States very much so I hope you won't think me very bold to write to such a great man as you are.

Have you any little girls about as large as I am if so give them my love and tell them to write to me if you cannot answer this letter. I have got 4 brothers and part of them will vote for you any way and if you will let your whiskers grow I will try and get the rest of them to vote for you; you would look a great deal better because your face is so thin. All the ladies like whiskers and they would tease their husbands to vote for you and then you would be president. My father is going to vote for you but I will try and get everyone to vote for you that I can I think that rail fence around your picture makes it look very pretty I have got a little baby sister she is nine weeks old and is just as cunning as can be. When you direct your letter direct it to Grace Bedell, Westfield, Chatauqua county, New York. I must not write any more answer this letter right off. Good bye.

GRACE BEDELL

Grace hardly expected a reply from so busy and important a man. But one day a letter with a Springfield, Ill., postmark landed in the Bedell mailbox. Written in "Old Abe's" own hand and dated Oct. 19, it read:

My dear little Miss: Your very agreeable letter of the 15th is received. I regret the necessity of saying I have no daughter. I have three sons—one seventeen, one nine, and one seven years of age. They, with their mother, constitute my whole family. As to the whiskers, having never worn any, do you not think people would think it a piece of silly affectation if I were to begin it now?

Your very sincere well-wisher,
A. LINCOLN

Her letter must have made an impression. For around election time his neighbors began to notice a little stubble on his chin. Some of them remonstrated. But when on Feb. 11 he bade farewell to Springfield and boarded a train for Washington to take the national helm in a time of desperate crisis for the Union, his beard was well grown.

His route lay through Westfield, where Chautauqua County's leading Republican, former Lieutenant Governor George W. Patterson boarded the Lincoln train. The President-elect asked Patterson if he knew a Bedell family living in Westfield. Of course the politico knew the Bedells—and every other family in his home town of Westfield. Lincoln told Patterson of the little girl's letter and added with a smile that lighted up his lined face: "You can see I have followed her suggestion."

At Westfield Lincoln made a little speech from the platform, as he did at most places along the way. He told the crowd of 2,000:

"Some three months ago, I received a letter from a young lady here. It was a very pretty letter, and she advised me to grow whiskers. Acting partly on her suggestion, I have done so. And now if Miss Grace Bedell is here, I would like to see her."

Grace was there, but away back in the rear of the crowd. She was dressed in her Sunday best. A neighbor had given her a bouquet of winter roses which she hoped to present to Lincoln. When the President-elect spoke her name, the crowd parted and she was thrust forward to the train.

The tall man stepped down from his car to a freight platform and the little girl was lifted up beside him. Lincoln bent over and kissed Grace on her cheek. Then as he straightened his long frame, he stroked his newly grown whiskers, saying gently:

"You see, I let these whiskers grow for you, Grace."

Then Lincoln stepped back into his car and the train pulled out for the Illinois politician's rendezvous with destiny.

Many years later, Grace recalled: "I was so embarrassed that I ran home as fast as I could, dodging in and out between horses and buggies and once crawling under a wagon. I completely forgot the roses that I was going to give the great man to whom I had offered such rare advice, and when I arrived home I had the stems, all that remained of the bouquet, still tightly clutched in my hand."

Grace was born in Orleans County. Her parents moved

to Westfield in the 1850s and returned to the Albion area shortly after the meeting with Lincoln.

Around 1868 Grace Bedell married George N. Billings of Carlton, a veteran of the Civil War who served with the 8th Heavy Artillery and was discharged as a sergeant in June of 1865.

Soon after their marriage the couple moved to Kansas, where Billings had taken a claim on land near what became the village of Delphos.

During the Kansas grasshopper plague of the 1870s, Mrs. Billings and her son, Harlow, spent a winter with her husband's family in Carlton, while he traveled to Arizona by mule team and wagon in search of work.

After the grasshoppers left the plains, the family was reunited in Kansas where George Billings for years was a teller of the State Bank of Delphos. The letter young Grace Bedell wrote to Lincoln in 1860 is still in possession of the family and in the keeping of the Delphos bank.

In 1930 the Abraham Lincoln Association sought out Grace Bedell Billings and brought her from Kansas, to be the surprise honor guest of the organization at its annual banquet at Springfield, Ill., on Lincoln's Birthday of that year. The famous historian, Allan Nevins, now chairman of the national Civil War Centennial Commission, was on the platform with her.

The guests at that banquet were delighted with the little old lady who liked to tell how the bearded Lincoln kissed her at the Westfield depot back in 1861.

Grace Bedell Billings died at Delphos in 1939, two days before her 91st birthday. She had been blind for 30 years.

Had it not been for the letter she wrote when she was a child of 11, the face on the schoolroom walls, in the history books, on our five dollar bills—and on our pennies—would be a smooth-shaven one.

Chapter 24

The "Lost" Flag

Civil War soldiers held for their regimental flags a sentimental regard that was akin to reverence. It was a disgrace to have one of the sacred banners fall into enemy hands.

This is the story of a Genesee Valley war flag which for years was generally believed to have been destroyed by its color bearer when Union troops were overwhelmed by Confederate forces at Cemetery Hill on the first day of the battle of Gettysburg.

By hiding the flag in his coat sleeve, a young Geneseo soldier saved the silken banner of the Wadsworth Guards, an action which went virtually unnoticed in the fury of the first clash of the Blue and the Gray in the crucial battle of the Civil War.

At war's end the Geneseo soldier brought the colors home with him—after he and the flag had spent three dreary months together in the Confederacy's notorious Libby Prison.

Nearly a century passed before the true story of the "lost" flag was made public, and now the 34-starred banner in its gilded frame is one of the prized Civil War relics in the Livingston County Historical Center at Geneseo, the gift of a grandson of the quick-witted soldier who had saved it.

Some history of the Wadsworth Guards is in order. At

the behest of the Valley's outstanding military figure, Gen. James S. Wadsworth, an infantry regiment was recruited in Livingston County in 1861.

It was named the Wadsworth Guards in honor of the general, the Valley grandee, who was to lose his life in 1864 in the battle of the Wilderness. The outfit trained under Col. John Rorbach at hastily-built Camp Union at the head of Geneseo's North Street.

The unit was mustered into service in January, 1862, at Albany as the 104th New York State Volunteers, with three companies added to the seven which had been raised in Livingston County.

After the regiment moved South, a silken flag, 18 by 24 inches, with the legend, "Wadsworth Guards, 104th N.Y.S.V." embroidered on two of its red stripes, was presented to the regiment by the wife of General Wadsworth at Catlett's Station, Va., in May of 1862.

Then came the morning of July 1, 1863, when two great armies collided, almost by chance, at a sleepy hill-girt Pennsylvania town named Gettysburg.

That historic morning found the 104th, attached to General Reynolds's I Army Corps, marching southward toward Gettysburg down the Emmitsburg Road. It got orders to reinforce Buford's dismounted cavalry, which had encountered a Confederate infantry column on a low ridge west of the village.

In mid-morning Reynolds's men went into action at Cemetery Hill. At first they beat back the Rebel attack. But Confederate reserves were rushed in under Generals A. P. Hill and Richard Ewell, until the Federals were outnumbered three to one.

Reynolds was killed, his outflanked corps was cut to pieces and forced to flee back through the town. The first round had been won by the Gray but the Rebel commander, Robert E. Lee, failed to follow up his initial success and the Wadsworth Guards were to come back and help Gen. George G. Meade repel the invaders.

It was at the height of the furious struggle for Cemetery Hill on July 1 that the color bearer of the Guards tried to destroy the regimental flag, fearing it would be captured by the enemy.

Young Sgt. John P. Welch snatched away the banner just in time and stuck it, neatly folded, into a sleeve of his coat. After the battle he sewed the silken flag into the coat lining with the needle and thread he always carried.

Welch later was captured and taken to Libby Prison at Richmond. No Rebel guard ever found the flag in his coat sleeve. When Welch entered Libby Prison, he weighed 150 pounds. When after three months he was freed in an exchange of prisoners, was down to 75 pounds.

After the 104th was mustered out, the sergeant and the flag came home to the Valley. For years the banner hung in Welch's farm home on the Lima Road in the Town of Geneseo. John Welch was a modest man and he never bragged about his exploit. Probably he did not think it of great significance. There were so many heroes and so many trophies around after the war.

Only his father and a few neighbors knew the story. It was generally believed, even by historians, that the color bearer of the Guards had destroyed the flag at Gettysburg.

When a grandson and namesake was born in 1911, the old veteran put the banner in its present frame and bequeathed it to the second John P. Welch.

In May, 1961, the first year of the Civil War centennial, the grandson of the veteran presented the flag to the Livingston County Historical Society. He was then in his last illness.

Miss Margaret E. Gilmore, Geneseo town historian and a long-time friend of the Welch family, obtained many facts about the flag from Mrs. Edward Welch, a daughter-in-law of the Civil War veteran who had sewed the emblem of "the Wadsworth Guards" into his coat sleeve nearly a century ago.

So now the silk banner that came back from the field of Gettysburg rests in the Historical Center, the embroidered legend on its stripes faded by the years. It is surrounded by swords, drums, uniforms, pictures and other reminders of the greatest war ever fought on this continent. It is part of the lore of the Valley.

Chapter 25

Grant's Indian

It was the hand of a man whose ancestors ruled this land long before the first white settler came that wrote the official copy of the document that, in effect, ended the Civil War.

That man was Ely Samuel Parker, military secretary to the Union commander, Gen. Ulysses S. Grant. He was a full blooded Seneca Indian born on a Western New York reservation and for some years a resident of Rochester.

After the vanquished Confederate chieftain, Robert E. Lee, had agreed to the terms Grant had scribbled on a piece of paper, it was the Indian aide who made interlineations in the penciled original draft and then in a clear hand transcribed the official copies of the articles of capitulation.

The date was April 9, 1865, and the scene was the parlor of a brick house at Appomattox, Va., the end of the road for the Lost Cause.

The rival commanders were a study in contrasts. General Lee, tall, stately, every inch the patrician, immaculate in a light gray dress uniform and carrying a jeweled sword, had one military aide at his side.

The victor, Grant, stubby, slouching, ill at ease in his rumpled blue private soldier's coat, without a sword, his boots spattered with mud and with only the stars on his shoulders to denote his rank, had arrived late with a half dozen staff officers.

Grant introduced them, one by one, to Lee. The Confederate leader took a second sharp look at the officer Grant presented as "Colonel Parker, my military secretary." At first the Southerner seemed to think the barrel-chested six footer with the sparse beard above a drooping mustache, long hair and dark skin was a Negro. Then he recognized Parker's features as unmistakably those of an American Indian.

General Lee extended his hand to Parker with the remark: "I am glad to see one real American here." The Indian replied with dignity: "We are all Americans."

Ely Parker was no ordinary reservation Indian. He was born to the tribal purple on the Cattaraugus Reservation near Gowanda in 1828. A grandnephew of the great Seneca orator, Red Jacket, he was the last grand sachem of the Iroquois Confederacy, the official "Keeper of the Western Door," an honor he held from 1852 until his death in 1895. His badge of office, a long, many-colored wampum belt, is now in the New York State Museum in Albany.

He was only 15 when he went to Washington as one of the representatives of his nation and, clad in buckskin, dined with President Polk in the White House.

Young Parker attended mission schools and spoke impeccable English. At the age of 22 he came to Rochester to further his education and became closely associated with Lewis Henry Morgan, the scholar who has been called "the father of anthropology."

When in 1851, Morgan published his *League of the Iroquois,* still considered the most authoritative work on the subject, the author acknowledged Parker's assistance in the preparation of the volume by dedicating it to the young Seneca.

After studying law for three years, Parker was denied admission to the bar by a Cattaraugus County judge's ruling that "Indians were non-citizens." Then he turned to civil engineering and after completing courses at the Rensselaer Polytechnic Institute, supervised work on the Erie Canal and other state waterways.

Parker lived in and around Rochester from 1850 to 1857. He was at one time ordnance officer of the old 54th Regiment of Rochester militia. Then he joined the government service as consulting engineer for the Upper Great Lakes Lighthouse District.

His work took him to Galena, Ill., where he made the acquaintance of a seedy, cigar-smoking newcomer to that town, U. S. Grant, a former Army captain who had left military service under a whiskey-lined cloud.

"Sam" Grant, as he had been known to his brother Army officers, had been a failure in everything he undertook after brilliant service in the Mexican War, and when he met Ely Parker in 1860, he was an ill-paid clerk in his brother's leather store in Galena. The two men formed an instant liking for each other.

The outbreak of the Civil War separated them for a while. Grant finally got a commission as colonel of an Illinois volunteer regiment. When the two friends met again, it was 1863 and Grant was a departmental commander with Forts Donelson and Henry and bloody Shiloh on his war record.

Meanwhile the Indian encountered many barriers in his efforts to win a commission in the Union army. The government refused to release him from his engineering duties until 1862. He was rebuffed at Albany and Washington, where he was told by a high official that "Indians should stay home and grow corn."

Nevertheless some 3,000 Indians were to fight for the

Union and Parker was responsible for recruiting more than 700 of his people.

At last, in June, 1863, he got his commission, in the engineering division. Three months later came the orders which reunited him with the friend he had made in Illinois. He joined Grant's command at Vicksburg and his work impressed the general.

After that he was on Grant's staff through the Tennessee campaign and had attained the grade of assistant adjutant general when his chief was given command of the reorganized Army of the Potomac.

The Indian was with Grant in the hell of the Wilderness and throughout the slow, dogged, blood-soaked Union drive toward Richmond.

On Aug. 20, 1864 he was made Grant's military secretary and promoted to lieutenant colonel. Parker had a gift for words and he wrote a neat hand. Grant signed many letters, reports and orders which his secretary had composed.

On the day of Lee's surrender, Ely Parker was commissioned a brigadier general of volunteers. In 1867 he was breveted in the regular army with that rank.

He resigned on April 29, 1869. Grant was now in the White House and he had one more job for his Indian friend to handle, the post of commissioner of Indian affairs. Parker was accused of corruption in the conduct of that office, but won full exoneration from a House investigating committee.

Then he resigned. He had had his fill of what he called "a thankless position" and expressed a desire to spend his "declining years in peace and quiet." His last position was as a supply clerk with the New York City Police Department.

Death came to General Grant's onetime military aide in 1895. Now he sleeps beside Red Jacket and others of his forefathers in Buffalo's Forest Lawn Cemetery.

The late Dr. Arthur C. Parker, longtime director of the Rochester Museum of Arts and Sciences, archeologist and historian, was a grandnephew of the Civil War veteran.

Ely Parker had been rebuffed as a "non-citizen" and told to "go home and grow corn." He lived to become a brilliant engineer and a member of the Union army's high command.

And it was fitting that in the historic drama at Appomattox the hand which inscribed the document which was to end the nation's long and gory fratricide was that of an original American.

Chapter 26

Drummer Girl?

Did a girl from the Finger Lakes area, masquerading as a man, beat a drum in the Union army in 1861?

In the files of the *Rochester Democrat and American* of Dec. 18, 1861 is a Page One story about "a smart-looking lad wearing a military cap and overcoat applying at the recruiting office of Capt. Benjamin in the Reynolds Arcade to enlist as a drummer."

The applicant told the recruiters she had served as a drummer boy for two months in the 18th New York Volunteers under the name of "Edward D. Hamilton." She said she was enamored of army life and was determined to re-enlist.

The newspaper account added that a "brief inspection in a private room" revealed that the "drummer boy" was a girl. It added that "she was provided with women's clothes and turned over to the police" and that she appeared before a magistrate who let her off with a rebuke.

The young woman claimed that she had enlisted in the 18th as a drummer in the spring of 1861 and after two months with that outfit, she was transferred to a Pennsylvania regiment where she served as an orderly to an officer. She said she had been discharged but did not explain whether it was because her masquerade had been penetrated.

After her court appearance in Rochester, she was returned to the home of her mother in Cayuga County, to whom supposedly she had sent her army pay. The newspaper did not reveal the girl's real name nor the address of the mother.

According to the newspaper, the career of this "drummer girl" had been anything but conventional. Dressed in man's clothes, she had driven hackney coaches in Rochester and Buffalo. She had traveled two years with a circus. Earlier in 1861 she had been in Rochester with a man who sold buggy whips from a wagon.

She was identified as the same person who had tended bar the previous winter at the Clinton House at Albion under the name of Charles Miller. After her sex was revealed, she was haled before a justice of the peace and ordered to leave town.

The newspaper said: "This woman is over 30. She claims to be 21. In crinoline she appears to be 25 or 26; in pantaloons only 17 or 18. Only her rather lady-like walk betrayed her."

The records of the 18th New York Volunteers, on file in Albany, show no "Edward D. Hamilton" on its roster. Still it is possible that when the "drummer's" masquerading was uncovered, her name was scratched from the rolls.

The 18th was mustered into service at Albany on May 13, 1861 under the command of Col. William A. Jackson. Of its eight companies, all were raised in the eastern part of the state except Company G, which was organized at Canandaigua. If the girl from Cayuga County ever got into the 18th at all, she most likely would have signed up with Company G.

The regiment left the state on June 19, 1861. It was stationed in Washington before being attached to the Army of Northeast Virginia on July 13. After taking part in minor battles in Virginia, it fought as part of the Army of the Potomac at Bull Run July 21.

Could the "girl drummer" have been with the 18th at Bull Run? It's highly improbable. In fact her whole story of service in the war is fantastic. Yet it might have happened.

One fact is indisputable: A girl masquerading as a young man tried to enlist as a "drummer boy" in Rochester in December, 1861.

Chapter 27

The Sourdoughs

In August, 1896, an obscure prospector discovered a rich vein of gold in the remote Yukon territory of Northwestern Canada. That strike, near the junction of the Yukon and Klondike Rivers, touched off America's last great gold rush, the stampede to the Klondike.

It was months before the electrifying news reached the outside world. Then a mighty stream of humanity began pouring into the new Eldorado. Between early 1897 and late 1898 an estimated 40,000 from this and other countries reached "the Promised Land." Thousands of others turned back.

Among the victims of "Klondike Fever" were scores from Central-Western New York. Few, if any of them, found their pot of gold at the end of the rainbow they pursued so ardently, although the Klondike made some millionaires.

The Argonauts of the 1890s brought back a wealth of lasting memories. To reach the land of buried treasure they faced fearful hardships. They forged a human chain across an icy, snow-swept, precipitous pass with its summit 4,000 feet above sea level. They built their cabins and boats of green lumber. They conquered—or bypassed— raging rapids. They endured intense cold and stifling heat.

They lived on scanty and monotonous rations. Not the least of the troubles of "the sourdoughs" were the mosquitoes.

They were called "sourdoughs" because much of the time they had to eat bread made of fermented dough kept from one baking to start the next, instead of beginning each time with fresh yeast.

The prospectors let their whiskers grow in the hot summer as protection against the "skeeters" and were smooth shaven in the bleak winters so their beards would not freeze. Most of them were in their 20s and 30s.

This is no place for old men or boys. Some leave early, sick and discouraged. Some die of typhoid fever, others in snow and rock slides. Some are frozen to death. The work is hard, the tent life rough. We eat like horses, sleep like snakes.

That grim picture of life in the Klondike was written in May, 1898 for the *Rochester Post Express* by prospector-correspondent A. L. Hitchings.

Batavia was a favorite "jumping off place" for Western New York "sourdoughs," although almost every other community in this part of the state was represented in the army of gold seekers.

Few, if any, of the Western New York "sourdoughs" are alive but there are many Klondike buffs. One of the most active of them is Clayton J. Scoins of East Pembroke. His hobby for years has been collecting the lore of the Klondike and he spent long hours talking with veterans of the gold rush before they passed on.

Scoins made the gold rush days come alive again in 1961 with an exhibit he produced in the historic Holland Land Office in Batavia. It is the result of long research and painstaking craftsmanship.

He has reproduced a full-size windlass and bucket such as the miners used to bring up the dirt from the shafts they dug. Often they had to build fires to thaw the frozen earth. When the weather broke, the dirt they had piled at the top of the shaft was shoveled into sluice boxes and the gold was washed from the sand and gravel.

Scoins also built a scale model boat of the type the prospectors used in navigating the lakes and rivers that led to the Klondike fields. His collection includes a Yukon stove, cooking utensils, stools, tables and tools of the kind that stood in miners' cabins.

In the Scoins collection are many rare pictures taken in 1898 by prospector John G. McJury of Batavia, a professional photographer, along with McJury's log, the diaries of other "sourdoughs" and newspaper clippings. Much of the material for this chapter was drawn from Clayton Scoins's treasure trove.

His files indicate that one of the earliest Western New York expeditions left Batavia on March 16, 1897. It was sparked by Daniel Fraser of Franklinville, Cattaraugus County, who as a boy had worked his way by boat to the Yukon country and was there when the first gold was struck.

Others in the party were Cleveland M. Gillett of South Byron, Albert G. Bauer of Byron Center, John Lee of Franklinville and Marlin Mosier, Robert Menzie and Edward Hutchinson, all of Caledonia. These men were in their twenties and thirties.

The seven left Buffalo for Seattle on a "Klondike excursion train," paying a fare of $25 each. The railroads reaped a rich harvest by running many such specials during the stampede.

The "sourdoughs" stocked up on provisions, sleds and

warm clothing in Seattle, whence they traveled by boat to Skagway in Alaska, the American gateway to the Klondike.

Then they hauled their gear by hand on sleighs to the foot of the formidable Chilkoot Pass, the shortest—and most perilous—route to the gold fields.

That 50-mile pass was caked with ice and buffeted by blinding snowstorms. In 1898 a slide there claimed 60 lives. Yet for two years an almost continuous human chain crawled up its hazardous slopes.

Marlin Mosier of Caledonia on his return from the Klondike in 1898 wrote of the Chilkoot Pass:

"We found it impossible to haul our sleighs by ordinary means. So we had 600 feet of rope, one end of which was fastened to a sleigh and then carried the other up the slope and passed it through a pulley fastened to a stake.

"In this way we were able to make 300 feet at a haul, four of us pulling at the rope while the sleigh went up. We finally found shelves where sleighs could be hauled by hand."

The Canadian government, which taxed each miner's outfit and also the gold he took out, allowed no one to enter Yukon Territory without a year's supply of food, about 500 pounds. This did not include his tools and other equipment. The average miner could pack only about 60 pounds.

So at points along the Pass, he had to cache the rest of his supplies and reclaim them later. The Canadian "Mounties," who had police posts all along the line, guarded the caches. Chilkoot Indians charged $1 a pound for packing a prospector's gear over the Pass.

The Western New Yorkers finally negotiated the Pass, then halted to whipsaw green timber into a cabin and a boat. The boat was 35 feet long, 3 feet wide at the bottom,

6 feet wide at the top with pointed ends and would hold seven persons and about 3,300 pounds.

When there was a breeze, the boatmen would hoist a sail. When it was calm, they had to row up the streams. They conquered the treacherous White Horse Rapids, bane of many an Argonaut.

The seven miners began operations along the Bonanza and the Eldorado where fabulous treasure was unearthed —but precious little of it on the Western New Yorkers' claims.

Sometimes their meal consisted of a piece of bread about three inches square and a chunk of moose meat of about the same size.

When they replenished their provisions in Dawson, the gold rush boom city which today is a ghost town, they paid dearly for them—$6 for a 50-pound sack of flour, 30 cents a pound for sugar and 50 cents a pound for oatmeal.

Mosier recalled that when his party left Dawson, homeward bound on Nov. 28, 1897, with nine dogs hauling their sleds, the mercury stood at 65 degrees below zero. The men picked their way across the ice, eating two meals a day until they reached American soil in Alaska and boarded a boat for the United States.

A second group of Klondikers, known as "the Batavia party," left that Genesee County shire town in February, 1898. H. H. Scott of Batavia was the leader or captain. Besides photographer-diarist McJury, other members were Alden R. Smith of Clifton Springs, Edwin Votry and George A. Anderson of Batavia, Wendell Prentice of Stafford and John D. Toll of Bethany. Toll turned back at Dyea, a gateway to the Klondike country, to join the Navy and was with Dewey's fleet at Manila Bay.

Here in capsule form is John McJury's log of the "Batavia party's" 17-months in a strange, far place.

Feb. 25, 1898—left Batavia.
March 12—arrived Skagway via Seattle.
March 14—sledded $3\frac{1}{4}$ miles to first camp.
April 3—not on trail. snow slides. many lives lost. (on the Chilkoot Pass.)
April 6—trail open and began packing over summit.
May 9—started cutting timber for boats at Lake Bennett.
May 11—first mosquitos.
May 21—three boats finished.
June 6—boats piloted through canyon and rapids.
July 2—arrived in Dawson—moose dinner $1.50—in line for mail.
July 14—boat swamped, lost cooking utensils.
July 19—prospecting.
July 30—chewed by gnats.
July 31—packed to Sulphur Creek, discovered gold on 17.
Aug. 9—building cabin, 90 degrees in shade.
Aug. 19—Scott shot five mountain grouse.
Aug. 21—picked cranberries.
Sept. 19—whipsawed lumber for cabins.
Oct. 1—C. Tyler passed away 5 a.m. from typhoid fever.
Oct. 17—after making buckets and windlass, started sinking shaft.
Dec. 24—Bob's cabin entertained, 36 present, dance and music. (Christmas Eve in the Klondike.)
Jan. 17, 1899—commenced sinking new shaft.
March 26—received two letters, my first mail.
Apr. 27—Sandy Roberts fell into shaft.
May 6—started sluicing.
May 13—found $20.50 nugget in sluice box.

May 31—funeral of Nelson, the Swede.

June 26—boarded the steamer *Nelson* at Skagway at midnight.

July 17—reached Seattle.

And the last entry:

July 23, 1899—arrived Salt Lake City, visited Fort Douglas.

* * *

Alden Smith, who was only 21 when he left the family farm near Clifton Springs for the Klondike, was one of the most popular members of the Batavia party. He was lively and full of jokes, and his partners dubbed him "Cy Haskins," after some now forgotten stage character or humorist of the time.

His family has preserved a valuable addition to the local lore of "the sourdoughs" in the form of letters he wrote home from the Yukon and the letters the home folks wrote him.

His messages from the Klondike add some human sidelights to the McJury log, and while the letters from the home folks told mostly about the crops and the neighborhood doings, they also revealed the intense interest the home front had in the progress of the Spanish-American War, which coincided with the second year of the big gold rush and did much to slow up the stampede to the Yukon.

Sometimes three months elapsed before the two-way letters reached their destinations and young Smith never received some of the mail from home. The Smith family farm was near the hamlet once called Plainsville, later Gypsum, on the Canandaigua Outlet, about two miles north of Clifton Springs.

Here are some excerpts from the young "sourdough's"

letters home, along with a few he received from Ontario County:

"Seattle, March 6, 1898—Some of the boys are a little homesick but I want to see that Klondike country. I suppose the talk is all war but we don't hear much about it. Most people here have not heard that the Maine was blown up."

"Sheep Camp, Alaska, March 20—We arrived here last night with our camp outfit. Our goods are at Canyon City two miles below. We passed through the canyon last night; it is two miles long and up hill all the way . . . with walls of rock on each side about 200 feet high. We have had fine weather ever since reaching Dyea, clear with sunshine and warm days and frosty nights. It would be good sugar weather if there were many maples, but the trees are all pine and willow. . . . The snow is about four feet deep here in our mountain camp.

. . . There was a man shot in Dyea. There was four of them in the racket, a lot of gamblers. . . . We see them all along the sled trail with their little canvas tables, trying to catch some sucker, but the men don't bite very well. . . . They caught the men that committed the murder in Dyea and sent them to Sitka for trial. There is not as much excitement about a murder here as there would be in Clifton over a dog fight. I carry my revolver when we move camp and that is about the only time I feel as safe as I did at home. If anyone minds his business here, he will get along. . . ."

An April 8 letter written from the foot of the awesome Chilkoot Pass described th disastrous snowslides on the Pass:

"They have found 53 dead and 16 more are missing above here. One man found his son dead in the snowslide.

We had a Masonic meeting and raised money to send home the bodies of two brothers who were killed. The trail was closed for three days so they could get out the dead."

The Batavia party safely negotiated the Pass which Smith described as "one jam of horses, mules, oxen, dogs and men. There are now thousands on the trail. Many have turned back since the fatal snowslide."

A letter in May when the miners were building cabins and boats at Lake Bennett prior to going up the waterways and shooting the foaming rapids told how "many a cheer went up when the men learned of Dewey's victory at Manila."

Smith also wrote disparagingly of an item of diet called "anchor pudding, which is made of bread dough and fruit and boiled in a pan of water until it's done. The boys said it is so heavy and soggy it would make a good anchor for the boat. . . . We sleep all right; we have a bed of boughs in one end of the tent and spread our blankets and robes on them and crawl under the top one, six of us in a row."

A June 30 letter from Indian River contained this nostalgic touch: "I suppose you are haying now. We are sinking some holes. We find some color but not of much amount."

Nearly three weeks later Alden received this news from his mother, in a letter postmarked June 20:

"We have planted 28 acres of corn and 80 acres of potatoes. Father and I cut all the seeds. We are getting ready to shear sheep tomorrow. The fruit crop is very promising. Admiral Sampson has the Spanish fleet bottled up in the harbor of Santiago."

On Independence Day Mrs. Smith proudly told of Sampson's "glorious victory" and added that: "Father, George and I will spend the Fourth at home. The hired men are all gone and Mary and Lura (Alden's sisters) are going to a picnic up Canandaigua Lake. We have been cutting and drawing hay. The wheat and barley are about ready to harvest."

So the young prospector, far from the familiar Ontario county countryside was kept posted—a bit belatedly—about world events and home doings. His sisters and other relatives wrote about local love affairs, law suits, deaths, illnesses and births in the neighborhood.

Meanwhile back at the camp—at Sulphur Creek—Alden was writing, "I am cook this week and have to bake bread. Oh, how these fellows do eat. I will throw pancakes into them for breakfast, beans and bacon for dinner; beans, bread and bacon for supper."

Of a visit to the fabulous Bonanza Creek where the first gold had been struck in 1896, Smith wrote:

"There are miles and miles of sluice boxes. The creek bottom looked as if it had been dug out pretty well. In many places the side hills are being worked. Men dig out the dirt while others wash it up with a rocker, carrying water from the creek in many places in pails."

On reaching Dawson city, he found "here it looks a little like civilization, with four large river steamers lying at the dock. A string of warehouses have been built and a dozen more have the frames up. Three sawmills are running night and day with the waterfront full of logs."

After receiving word from home that "Mr. Cotton got hurt by a bull," Smith wrote of a man who "got his coat torn off by a bear on Gold Bottom Creek. He was fooling with a cub and the old lady made a pass at him. His coat was hanging over his back and the she bear caught it and all he had left was pieces . . . he got out of the gulch fast. . . . We have a good many cranberries here, some currants and blueberries."

Sadness over a death and longing for home were mingled in an October letter from Sulphur Creek: "One of the boys across the creek, Charles Tyler of Byron, died of typhoid fever this morning. . . . You are picking apples and digging potatoes now. I am not homesick—but I would like to get a letter today. My latest was dated June 25."

A homespun letter from a cousin, Asa Smith, written from Clifton in July, wondered if "you don't get rather lonesome up there for the society of good girls and no horses to care for in the morning, cows to milk, pigs to feed, ducks to water."

Cousin Asa's comment on foreign affairs: "Spain has just asked for terms of surrender. She had better quit now . . . McKinley is a dandy and no mistake. The only snag now is what will we do with our new white elephant, the Philippines. We don't want them and can't give them away without making trouble in Europe. They are not capable of governing themselves."

Up in the Klondike, things were looking up in November. "Our prospects are very good. Some of the dirt will show up $1.10 to the pan. It is from 40 to 50 below zero."

The next letter from the Klondike told how "dog sleds bring the grub from Dawson, 40 miles up grade. Sleds stick to the snow but the dogs will pull as if for life. A dog can get hold of the trail with his nails. The buckskin moccasins we wear are pretty smooth. If people up here were to wear tight boots or shoes as they do down East, their feet would be frozen. I suppose you are all done with the fall's work and thinking of killing hogs now. Fresh pork is $1 a pound in Dawson."

As the Christmastide neared, Alden Smith, despite his insistence that he "wasn't homesick," wrote home:
"I wonder what the folks will be saying about the one

who is up here under the Circle with the Northern Lights over his head."

That was his last letter from the Yukon in the historic year of 1898 which saw the ebbtide of the human flood to the goldfields and which brought the United States an easy victory over decrepit Spain and made this nation a world power.

Young Smith's letters in 1899 indicate an increasing disenchantment with the "Promised Land" of gold. In February he wrote:

". . . I suppose everybody on the outside thinks everybody up here is going to be rich in a short time. The estimate of last year's output of gold dust in the Yukon was $7 million. As there are now in the Klondike an estimated 15,000 to 18,000 miners, it figures out that each will get about $466.66, not enough to buy grub."

On May 14 he wrote that "our dirt is not turning out as good as we expected but we got a nugget yesterday worth $20.50." The Batavia party was preparing to return to the States when in June young Smith received this message from home:

"There is lots of good digging and good dirt in the fields north of the house and you can dig out nuggets of potatoes and gather bushels of golden grain on the surface." It was signed "Mother."

By late July, 1899, Alden Smith was back home on the farm. He kept in touch with his old comrades of gold rush days until his death in 1920.

One of his letters home mentioned "the ladies up here. There are a good many of them on the trail. They wear men's pants and coats and rubber boots. You could hardly tell them from the men if their long hair did not give them away." He did not elaborate and his casual reference to "the ladies on the trail" prompted me to ask Clayton

Scoins for further information about the women in the Klondike.

Scoins estimates that about three out of every 100 on the trails were women, most of them with their husbands. He knew of no instance where any woman actually dug for gold. But quite a few owned claims and had miners work them on a 50-50 sharing basis. Generally speaking, owners lived in cabins on their claims. Scoins recalled that at least two women lost their lives in the Chilkoot Pass snowslide disaster.

He believes no more than 5 per cent of the women in the Klondike could be called "camp followers." Dawson City had its brothels, dance halls and saloons, but Scoins feels that the picture of the boom town as "a sin capital" has been overdrawn.

Many men, accompanied by their wives, went to the Yukon during the gold rush, not as miners, but to become merchants, professional men, mechanics and to provide other services in the newly developed territory. Besides a number of show girls, mostly vaudeville performers who went to the Klondike, were many nurses, cooks, missionaries, waitresses, seamstresses and the like. Some of them remained in the territory after the gold rush had ended.

Which would seem to account for the many "ladies on the trail."

* * *

Several Rochesterians took part in the stampede to the Klondike. When in August, 1897, the steamer *Mexico* struck a rock near Sitka, Alaska, and sank, among the 400 passengers and crew members who were saved by taking off in life boats were Mr. and Mrs. Frank Dennis of Rochester. Their experience was described as "harrowing." The news story, while stating that many of the passengers were pros-

179

pectors, did not disclose what the Rochester couple was doing in Alaska at the time.

Late in 1897, Jacob H. Myers of Rochester, inventor of the first voting machine used in New York State, and his son, Dr. Oscar, left for the Yukon. The son wrote in April, 1898, of their building a cabin on the Bonanza Creek, where the first gold strike had been made in 1896, of the dog teams that carried the mail and of the lucky prospectors who made rich strikes near the Myers claim.

Another Rochester party, headed by Dr. Frederick R. Smith, a prominent physician, headed north in 1898. It was well equipped and maintained a large "stable" of dogs. But no account of sudden riches won by this expedition was recorded.

"Klondike Fever" spawned many "get rich quick" stock companies. Considerable Western New York money was sunk in such wildcat schemes.

As for the Rochester adventurers, they might better have stayed at home and put their money in George Eastman's growing industry.

When first they returned from the Klondike, with little to show for their months of hardship, the former "sourdoughs" were generally loath to talk about their adventures. But time tempered their disillusionment and there came a day when they were happy to get together and share their memories of the Yukon.

In 1915 Western New York veterans of the gold rush formed a Klondike Clan and held their first reunion. There was another the next year. Then the first World War suspended the get-togethers, usually held in or around Batavia, until 1921. Then they were resumed and continued until well into the 1940s. In the later years the Clan added to its rolls anyone who had lived in Alaska or the Yukon, even after the gold rush had long been over.

A dozen years after the Klondike gold rush, Robert W. Service began writing poems and ballads about the Yukon and the "sourdoughs." His *Spell of the Yukon* includes this stanza:

> *There's a land where the mountains are nameless,*
> *And the rivers all run God knows where;*
> *There are lives that are erring and aimless,*
> *And deaths that just hang by a hair.*
> *There are hardships that nobody reckons;*
> *There are valleys unpeopled and still.*
> *There's a land—oh, it beckons and beckons,*
> *And I want to go back—and I will.*

But few of the Upstate "sourdoughs" who crawled over the Chilkoot Pass, who froze in Winter and baked in Summer, who fought mosquitos and typhoid fever, who buried their dead in the wilds and came home, nearly empty-handed, shared the poet's nostalgia for "the beckoning land."

Still they had rich memories of an unforgettable experience and they played their roles in a dramatic chapter of history—America's last great gold rush.